Y0-BRM-721

BY CHRISTINA SOONTORNVAT

ILLUSTRATED BY KEVIN HONG

Scholastic Press / New York

Library of Congress Cataloging-in-Publication Data available

ISBN 978-1-338-75917-4

10 9 8 7 6 5 4 3 2 1   23 24 25 26 27
Printed in Italy 183

First edition, July 2023
Book design by Cassy Price

For the Bulldogs of Brentwood Elementary

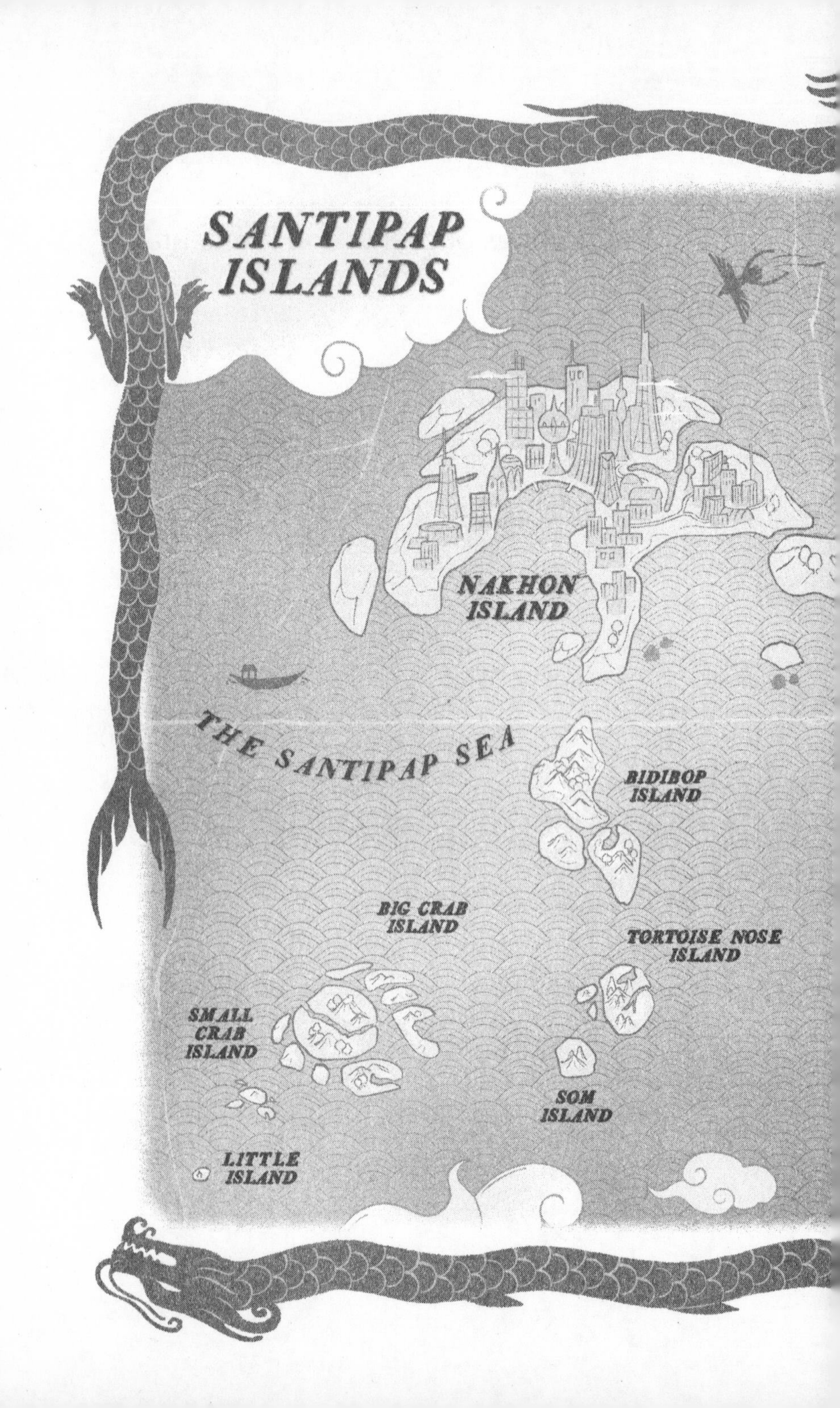
SANTIPAP ISLANDS
NAKHON ISLAND
THE SANTIPAP SEA
BIDIBOP ISLAND
BIG CRAB ISLAND
TORTOISE NOSE ISLAND
SMALL CRAB ISLAND
SOM ISLAND
LITTLE ISLAND

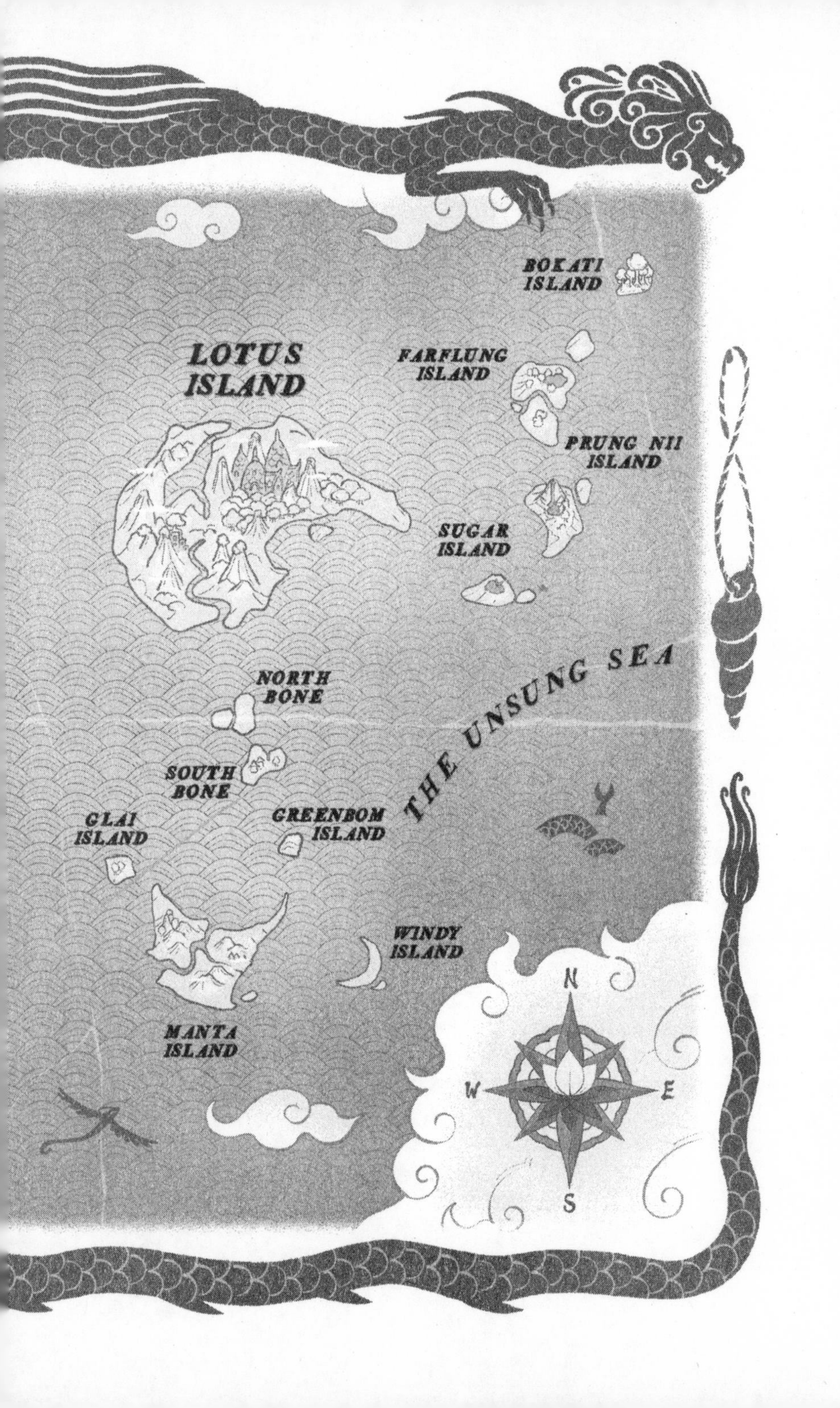
BOKATI ISLAND
LOTUS ISLAND
FARFLUNG ISLAND
PRUNG NII ISLAND
SUGAR ISLAND
THE UNSUNG SEA
NORTH BONE
SOUTH BONE
GLAI ISLAND
GREENBOM ISLAND
WINDY ISLAND
MANTA ISLAND
N
W
E
S

Cherry elbowed me in the ribs and pointed up into the branches of the pomelo trees. "I told you. They're finally ripe!"

When your name is Plum and your best friend is a girl named Cherry, I guess it's only natural that you'd spend a lot of your time thinking about fruit.

My mouth watered when I saw the plump pomelos swinging on their stems. I know what waited inside the thick rinds: juicy jewels of sweetness. It was still early morning and we hadn't eaten breakfast yet. "Wow, I can't believe the other Novices haven't found these," I said.

"They're all ours," murmured Cherry. "I mean, of course we'll share what we bring back."

"Oh, of course," I said with a grin. "*After* we stuff our faces."

Cherry rubbed her hands together and licked her lips. "Now, let's get picking!" With a wink, she began her transformation.

Fluffy cream-colored fur burst out all over her arms and legs, and her hands widened into paws. Her face elongated into a bear snout with a wet black nose. And she grew big, big, and bigger still.

As soon as she was fully transformed, I threw my arms around her belly and hugged her.

"Hey," said Cherry. "That's too tight!"

I smooshed my face into her fur. "I can't help it! When you're a gillybear, you're just so fluffy and huggable!"

"Okay, okay," said Cherry, pushing me away. "A gilly-bear is a ferocious fighter, not some squishy toy, you know. Besides, this fur is way too hot for hugs today. We've got to get these pomelos before I sweat to death!"

She rose up on her back legs and reached for the branches. The lowest pomelos hung too high for her to reach, even when she hopped.

I placed my hand on the smooth tree trunk. "Dear Auntie Pomelo, could you please make it just a teensy bit easier for us to reach your fruit?"

The pomelo tree's leaves rustled. It sounded a little bit like laughter, if trees could laugh. And then I swore those branches lifted *up* and farther away.

Cherry put her paws on her hips and gave me an annoyed look.

"Hey, it's not my fault pomelo trees have a mocking sense of humor!" I said.

"Will you at least transform and help me out here?"

I sighed. "Fine."

I took a deep breath and reached my hands down to the ground. This motion always helped me transform into my Guardian form. My arms and legs stretched long and my neck stretched tall as I became a roan: a deerlike creature with ruby-red antlers.

"Great, now give me a boost," said Cherry.

I crouched low so Cherry could put a foot on my back and boost herself up. She leaned her paw on the top of my head for balance.

"A little higher," said Cherry. "Almost there . . . hey, watch those pokey antlers!"

"Oof, are you done yet?" I grunted. I wiggled and squirmed underneath Cherry, trying to hold still. How had I let her talk me into this again?

At that moment, I looked up and saw a fuzzy inchworm

dangling from a strand of silk that hung down from the branches. The plump little worm squirmed and wiggled in the air. I smiled to myself, thinking I must look a lot like that.

And then I thought about how Cherry and I were connected just like that inchworm was connected to its tree. If she needed me—even if it meant looking like a silly, squirming larva—I'd be there for her.

Suddenly I had a strange zinging feeling that ran from the tips of my antlers through my whole body. I felt a tug on my heart as if Cherry and I really *were* connected by an invisible thread. I shut my eyes, and I could actually imagine a strand of silk running from me to her.

"There we go, Plum!" said Cherry. "I can reach them!"

Cherry stepped off of me. I could still feel the tingling in my antlers. I looked at Cherry and gasped.

She reached up into the high branches easily without even standing on her tiptoes. I shook my head and looked again. Could it be?

She was four feet taller than she had been a moment ago.

"Aw yeah, pomelos galore!" Cherry was not only taller but stronger too. She plucked a massive pomelo from its thick stem as easily as if it were a grape.

"Cherry, you're . . . you're enormous!"

"'Course I am," she said as she plucked fruit after fruit.

"No, I mean you're—"

But then the tingling in my antlers faded away, and I saw Cherry shrink and shrink until she was back to her usual gillybear size. By then she had gathered a dozen of the precious fruits.

I blinked and shook my head again. Was I seeing things?

Cherry didn't seem to have noticed anything out of the ordinary.

"Do you feel okay?" she asked. "You have a weird look on your face."

"I just saw you grow . . . big."

"Hey, getting big is part of my Guardian power." She

flexed her bear muscles. "Size, strength, and agility. Don't forget the agility part. Very important in wrestling. Speaking of . . ." She transformed back into her human form. "We should get going. I plan to beat Mikko in wrestling today, and I need to warm up."

I nodded and transformed back into my human form too.

With our arms full of pomelos, we bowed to the tree.

"Thank you, Auntie Pomelo," I said.

"Yeah, thanks for nothing," muttered Cherry.

At that moment, a big fat pomelo dropped from the branch and thumped right onto her head, making her drop all her fruit to the ground.

I chuckled as I helped Cherry pick them up. "I told you, pomelo trees have a sense of humor. You kind of asked for that."

The pomelo leaves rustled their laughter as we made our way out of the grove and down the hill.

The sun had risen higher over the horizon, and the whole of Lotus Island stretched out before us. The sheer gray cliffs cast shadows over the classroom buildings of the Guardian Academy. I could see the big kitchen garden and, down near the sea, the wide Lotus Court with its three circular ponds full of fragrant flowers.

The low gong of a bell rang out across the valley.

Cherry and I looked at each other, then bolted down the hill. For all of us Novices, there were two unspoken rules at the Guardian Academy:

Expect the unexpected.

And do not show up to class late.

After Cherry and I stashed the pomelos in our dorm room, I rushed to change into my Novice uniform: a pale green tunic and pants. I was proud to have earned the right to wear this color. When we'd first arrived on Lotus Island a few months ago, I had been sure I'd never be selected to be a Novice. But at the last minute, I'd figured out how to transform into my roan form, passing my first test. If all went well with my training, I'd graduate with the other Novices in one year and become a full Guardian, working to protect all life throughout our islands.

But that was a big *if.*

"See you at lunch!" called Cherry as she ran out the door to her defense class with Master Dew.

Our other roommate, Hetty, had already left for her first meditation class of the day with our headmaster, Master Sunback.

Each Novice Guardian had their own special powers that fell into one of three types:

Breath Guardians learned to control their powers of the mind and senses.

Hand Guardians sharpened their powers of strength and agility.

And Heart Guardians—like me—worked to strengthen their healing powers.

At least that was what we were *supposed* to do.

I forced my feet to hurry down the dirt path that led to the barn where we met for our Heart classes. Inside the barn, I checked on our injured animals.

"Good morning, babies," I cooed to the orphan pipi chicks in their crate beneath the heat lamp. "And how are you, Grandpa Tortoise? Oh good, the crack in your shell is much smaller! And what's that, Miss Salazander? Your tail is growing back? Excellent!"

If all I had to do was hang out with these animals, I would be a perfect Heart Guardian. But I was supposed to be learning how to *heal* them. And I totally stank at that.

I reached inside my collar and pulled out my necklace: a

coiled shell on a string of twine. My mother had made it for me when I was a baby, before she and my dad had been lost at sea.

"Mother," I whispered, squeezing the shell tight, "I know you are with me, even though I can't hear your voice."

I *had* heard her voice once, speaking to me from inside the shell. That day she had told me her dream for me: to become a Guardian. Whenever I felt discouraged in class, I reminded myself that I had to keep trying. I had to make her dream come true.

"Hey, Plum, how are all your friends?"

I turned to see Salan coming through the barn door. Salan was one of the Novices from big Nakhon Island. Most of the other Novices from Nakhon Island teased me about talking to the animals, but Salan never joined them. And even though he was the best student in our Heart classes, for some reason he didn't mind being my partner for assignments.

Brass chimes rang out sweetly, the signal that class was about to start. Brother Chalad, our Heart teacher, greeted us in his Guardian form: a lemon-colored kinkajou with a fluffy tail. He seemed agitated, hopping from one little foot to the other.

"Good morning, Novices," said Brother Chalad. "There's been a slight change in today's schedule. Instead of our usual lesson, we will be putting everything you have learned so far to work with some of our island's most sacred living things: the lotus blossoms. Come, follow me."

Brother Chalad led our group out to the Lotus Court, a wide stone courtyard that looked out onto the sea below. In the center of the courtyard, lotus blossoms of every color floated in three large circular ponds.

Right away I could see why our healing skills were needed here. The dark green lotus pads bobbed on the surface of the water, and the blossoms reached for the sun. But at the edges of the ponds, the lotus pads were speckled with dry brown spots. Some of the lotus buds hung limply on pale stalks.

Brother Chalad demonstrated our task for the day. He knelt at the edge of one of the ponds and scooped up some water in his furry kinkajou hand. He sprinkled the water onto a speckled lotus pad. Then he placed his palm on the leaf and breathed out slowly. After a moment, vibrant green life began to flow out from the center of the leaf, erasing the brown spots one by one.

"Thank goodness," he whispered with a sigh of relief.

Then he looked up at us and quickly put on a smile. "You see? Nothing to it. Work with your partners. I'll come around and check on your progress."

I crouched beside Salan at the pond's edge and turned over a spotted lotus pad.

"What do you think is wrong with them?" I asked.

"I don't know," said Salan. "The sun isn't too hot today, so it can't be that. Should we start here?"

Salan transformed into his Guardian form: a bright blue wybird with a tuft of head feathers and wings that stretched as wide as I was tall. He got right to work, fanning his wings gently over the injured lotus. Bit by bit, green color slowly flowed back into the pads. The stalk thickened and the lotus bud gradually grew plump again.

"Gosh, Salan, you're so good at that. How do you do it?"

He smiled and shrugged. "It's just a feeling I get inside. Like when you play the right note on a piano. When you're doing it right, it just kind of . . . clicks."

I took a deep breath. *Nothing to it, Plum. You've got this.*

I transformed into my roan form and bent my antlers toward a damaged lotus bud. I shut my eyes and breathed in and out, focusing on everything that Brother Chalad had taught us. I waited and waited for the click Salan had described. But even though I didn't feel it, I did feel the lotus reaching out. It was weak and tired. It needed something. Something important. But what?

"Sweet lotus," I whispered, "please let me help you get better. Tell me what you need."

The stalk seemed to straighten up a little more, but then it sagged again. This was so frustrating! I could speak to the lotus all day, but no matter how hard I tried, I could not heal it.

"Keep it up, everyone," called out Brother Chalad. "I'll come check your progress now."

Beside me, Salan had his eyes closed, lost in his work. He was so good at healing. He could probably restore the whole pond by himself if he had enough time.

I suddenly had a strange idea. That morning, Cherry had grown bigger and stronger somehow. Had it been because of me? And if so, could I do it again?

I reached out with my hoof and gently touched the tip of Salan's wing. I shut my eyes.

Nothing happened. Hmm. What had I been doing when Cherry had grown? I had been thinking of the inchworm and being connected to my friend.

I shut my eyes tighter and imagined that an invisible thread ran between Salan and me.

My antlers zinged, just like before. I opened my eyes.

The lotus beneath Salan's wings glowed a vibrant green. The brown spots melted away. All the buds plumped up and filled out. Within seconds, the entire pond was thrumming with life. And just in time too.

Brother Chalad walked up to us. "My goodness, Salan and Plum! This is marvelous work!"

Salan opened his eyes and looked surprised. "Oh, wow! Plum, did you heal all of these?"

"I, um . . . I guess so, kind of?"

Salan fluttered his wings. "That's wonderful! You finally got the hang of it!"

Brother Chalad patted my shoulder. "Fantastic, Plum! What changed this time?"

I gulped. "I'm not sure. I guess it all just . . . clicked."

"Well, this is a great accomplishment, and you are on your way to becoming an excellent Heart Guardian. You should be proud of yourself!"

I could feel Salan smiling at me, but I couldn't look at him.

I wasn't proud at all. I hadn't healed those plants. I'd used Salan to do it.

When it came to being a Heart Guardian, I was a total fraud.

CHAPTER 3

Lunch was usually my favorite part of the day on Lotus Island. But today I wasn't hungry, and I felt too tired to talk to anyone.

As soon as Heart class was over, I slipped away from the other Novices. Quickly I made my way toward our dorm. But instead of going inside, I went around to the back of the building and found the hidden path that led into the shady forest. I followed the path around old trees studded with orchids, deeper into the forest until I finally arrived at a small muddy pond filled with white lotus flowers.

I walked past the pond and up the steps of a crumbling temple. I breathed in the scent of mossy stone.

Cherry and Hetty had been with me on the day we

discovered these ruins—our first day on Lotus Island. But since that day, they had gotten so busy with Novice training that they must have forgotten about them. Rella had been with us that day too.

I felt my face get hot the way it always did when I thought about Rella.

She was a girl from Nakhon Island who had never liked me for some reason. She had made everything between us a competition from day one. My life should have been easy now that she was gone. Instead I found myself thinking about her all the time. One thing was for sure—she never would have forgotten this place.

Inside the temple, I ran my hand over the cool stones. The walls were painted with a large mural that depicted the legend of the Guardians.

Long ago, when the world was young, our people had lived in a wonderful place called the Old Home. Animals, magical beasts, and humans lived in harmony under the loving gaze of the world's oldest and most powerful being: the Great Beast.

But humans began to destroy the Old Home with their greed and fighting. To escape the destruction, the Great Beast loaded all the animals onto his back, along with a few loyal humans. He swam away to the other side of the world.

At the end of his journey, he was so tired that he lay down in the sea and his body became our new home, the Santipap Islands. He gave the last of his power—from his breath, his heart, and his hands—to the humans who had come away with him. These people became the first Guardians, sworn to protect all life in the islands.

Along the bottom of the temple mural were golden letters written in curling script. They looked like decorations, but they were actually ancient chants. Rella had shown them to me and told me that if you spoke the words just right, you could immediately tap into the power of the Guardians. Instead of following the lessons of our master teachers, Rella had used these chants to help her transform into her Guardian form.

But the chants were a shortcut, one that Master Sunback said could be dangerous. Rella hadn't listened, and so she'd had to leave Lotus Island.

I had been tempted to use the chants too, and I had spoken them aloud just once. In the end I had decided not to use them to pass my transformation test. My transformation had happened just in the nick of time, and I had done it the right way. So I wasn't like Rella—was I?

I ran my fingers across the golden letters. My tongue shaped the words inside my mouth.

I shook my head and took a step back. I had to get out of there. I turned my back on the painted mural and walked out of the temple, into the sunlight. I followed the sound of trickling water to the small pond of lotus flowers.

What if saying the ancient chants that one time had done something bad to me? What if my powers had gotten messed up in some way? Maybe that explained why I was still the only Novice in my Heart class who couldn't heal anything. And now I had this new weird ability to affect the powers of my friends.

I sighed. "What is wrong with me?"

"Well, you're probably hungry, for one thing," said a voice behind me.

I turned and jumped when I saw a huge creature with a sable coat: half dog, half wolf.

"Sam, you scared me!"

The dog transformed into a tall boy with a bashful grin and glasses. "Sorry. Sometimes I forget how quiet I am when I'm in my wolfhund form."

"How did you know I was here?"

Sam tapped his nose. "Remember?"

Oh, right. Sam's Guardian powers were his super senses of smell and hearing.

I shoved my hands in my armpits. "I really hate when you say you can smell me."

"Hey, is that any way to say thank you?" He held out a shiny dark packet. "Here, I brought you lunch."

I took the packet from him and unwrapped the moist banana leaf, revealing steaming rice and sweet potato inside. Suddenly I was starving.

Sam and I sat at the edge of the pond while I scarfed down the food.

"This must be where you disappear to when I can't find you," said Sam, looking around. "It's a peaceful place to think. So . . . is everything okay?"

When I'd first arrived here, if you had told me that Sam Ubon would become one of my closest friends, I never would have believed it. Sam was the son of Lady Ubon, the wealthy, powerful ruler of Nakhon Island. I wondered if his mom would approve of him being friends with a farm girl like me. But Sam never looked down on me, and he was one of the best listeners I knew.

As I ate my lunch, I found myself telling Sam all about how I still wasn't able to do my Heart lessons. I left out the part about tricking Salan into doing our last assignment. I still felt bad about it.

"You should talk to Master Sunback," said Sam. "Tell her you're having trouble."

"Oh, sure, I'll tell our headmaster I haven't learned anything at her Academy," I said, rolling my eyes. "No way. What if she kicks me out?"

"She wouldn't do that," said Sam. He tapped my forehead in the space where my antlers grew. "You're a Novice. I was there when you transformed for the first time—or have you forgotten already?"

"Yeah, I guess," I mumbled.

Maybe Master Sunback wouldn't kick me out for doing poorly in class. But would she kick me out if she knew I had once spoken the chants?

"Don't be so hard on yourself," said Sam kindly. "Everyone has trouble in class now and then."

I sat back. "Oh yeah? What did *you* do in your Breath class today?"

Sam blushed. "I heard a caterpillar munching a leaf from one hundred yards away."

I couldn't help but laugh. "See? Everyone is moving ahead

of me. I can talk to the eggplant in the garden and the pipi chicks and the worms. But that isn't going to get me very far as a Guardian. The rest of you will go out into the world and protect it while I stay behind and tend the vegetables."

"Well, at least we'll always have eggplant waiting for us when we get back from saving the world."

I punched him gently in the arm for that—but not *too* gently.

"Ow! Hey, you just need a break from the routine." Sam got a glimmer in his eye. "Lucky for you, we're all getting one."

"What do you mean?"

Sam stood up and held his hand out to me. "If you weren't so busy moping around this muddy pond, you'd already know. Come on, everyone else is down at the dock. I'll let them tell you the news."

CHAPTER 4

Down at the beach, the blue mail boat was pulled up to our dock. The other Novices were crowded around, receiving packages.

My heart hopped like a cricket. Had Grandma and Grandpa sent me a letter? I missed them and our little farm so much! I even missed our rascally velvet goat, Tansy.

But instead of a letter, the mail carrier handed me a soft package wrapped in brown paper. That was a surprise. The kids from Nakhon Island got packages regularly, but my grandparents couldn't afford the postage.

I started to unwrap the paper when someone slapped my hand.

"Ow!" I looked up to see Hetty scowling at me. "Hey! What was that for?"

"We're not supposed to open them yet," said Hetty with a flip of her hair. "Master Dew's orders."

Mikko ambled over, rattling his package near his ear. "Master Dew didn't say we couldn't shake them."

"You're going to get in trouble!" said Hetty.

"What are the packages for?" I asked.

Hetty rolled her eyes. "For our field study, of course."

Cherry bounced toward us. "I hope my field study is on Farflung Island! They have wild burnberries growing everywhere!"

"Will someone *please* explain what the heck a field study is?" I cried.

"All the Novices are taking field trips away from Lotus Island next week," said Sam. "We'll study with different Master Guardians and learn all sorts of new things."

Master Dew, our defense teacher, clapped her hands as she walked out onto the beach. "All right, Novices, listen up, please! You have all been doing excellent work with your lessons here at the Guardian Academy. But the Master teachers on Lotus Island can only teach you so much. There are many more things for you to learn out in the wider world. The next test you must pass in your Guardian training will take place on a different island in our archipelago."

I felt a shiver of nervousness. Our first test had been so hard. I had barely passed it. What would this next test be?

Master Dew continued, "During your field study, your Master Guardian will teach you lessons and give you assignments. You must complete them all before you return home. The packages you hold in your hands contain items that will help you along the way. Now, I'll call out your names and tell you your field study placements. When I do, you may open your packages."

Cherry leaned close to me. "Isn't this so exciting?"

I nodded. I had hardly ever visited any other islands in the Santipap Archipelago. I couldn't wait to learn where I would be assigned.

Master Dew held up a piece of paper and began reading out names. "Basil and Twist! You are assigned to Master Soraiya on Sugar Island."

Basil and Twist squealed with glee and opened their packages. They held up broad straw sun hats.

"You'll need those," said Master Dew. "Sugar Island is legendary for its beautiful pink-sand beaches."

"Emmie and Drum, you are assigned to Manta Island."

The two of them ripped into their packages.

"Mittens!" they shouted.

Master Dew nodded. "Manta is the only island in our whole archipelago that gets snow. Those mittens will come in handy."

Another group of students was assigned to explore the glittering caves of Prung Nii Island. Another trio was off to Tortoise Nose Island, the island of one hundred waterfalls.

"Oh man," whispered Mikko. "I was really hoping to get that one!"

"Don't worry," said Sam. "You'll get assigned somewhere else cool."

"Hetty, Cherry, and Plum," called Master Dew.

The three of us clasped hands.

"You were assigned to Glai Island, home of the rare lavender fluff bunnies . . ."

We gasped with delight!

". . . but unfortunately a storm destroyed their boat dock, so you won't be going there after all."

We sagged.

"Instead you'll be joining Salan, Sam, and Mikko on their field study."

"Oh, well, that's fun news!" I said.

“Sure is,” said Cherry, high-fiving the boys.

But when Master Dew said “The six of you will study with Master Em on Bokati Island,” no one cheered or clapped. I had never heard of Bokati Island. From the confused looks on the other Novices’ faces, they hadn’t either.

Master Dew said, “Well? Don’t you want to open your packages?”

I peeled back the brown paper and pulled out . . .

“An itchy sweater?” said Hetty, holding up a pale gray bolt of wool.

“It’s a cloak!” said Master Dew. “You’ll be glad for that on Bokati Island. It’s quite chilly there. And damp. Very, very damp, actually.”

The other Novices giggled and ran off, chatting about all the sledding, swimming, and waterfall jumping they were planning to do.

“Is it just me, or does Bokati Island sound kind of gloomy?” asked Salan.

“I have to admit I’m a bit disappointed,” said Mikko.

“I’ll say,” whimpered Hetty.

Cherry threw her arms around us. “Hey, no grumpy faces! At least we’ll be together, right?”

I held up the cloak and smelled it. It wasn’t itchy at all. It was soft and smelled like sweet flour. I smiled. It was woven from the wool of dough sheep.

I wondered. Maybe it was like Sam said—maybe taking a break from Lotus Island would be good for my powers. But what if it made things worse?

Sam was right about something else too.

I couldn't put it off any longer.

I needed to talk to our headmaster, Master Sunback.

CHAPTER 5

Master Sunback was always easy to spot. Her short white hair was like a puffy cloud floating above her head. I found her walking the paths of the meditation garden, placing each step carefully.

I hung back. She looked like she was thinking about something really deep. Maybe this wasn't a good time.

I turned around and started to tiptoe away.

"Leaving already, Plum?"

I slowly turned back around and bowed to her.

"Sorry for disturbing you, Master Sunback. I'm sure you were meditating on something very important."

She nodded. "I was thinking about how this moss is

squishy, like tofu. Very important stuff. Now, what can I help you with?"

I cleared my throat. "Well, I was thinking about something. When Rella was kicked out of the Guardian Academy—"

Master Sunback held up one finger. "Not kicked out. She made the decision to do something that required her to leave. I never wanted her to go."

"Yes, okay. Well, you told me she had to leave because she used a forbidden method of transformation—"

"Rella was looking for a shortcut," said Master Sunback sadly. "All the lessons we teach you in class are important—not just for being a Guardian but for being a person in the world. Rella never took the time to learn. She wanted to be a Guardian so badly, but she didn't want to put in the work to get there."

"The method Rella used to transform—is it forbidden because it's *bad*? What I mean is . . . if someone used it, could it damage them? Like, forever?"

Master Sunback tilted her head back and forth like she wasn't sure. "What Rella did was very dangerous. There are things on this island that are so old—older than me, older than any Guardian alive today. Not even I understand them completely. I had to send Rella away because I didn't want her to get hurt." She put one hand on my shoulder. "Plum, I can tell you are concerned about your friend. But Rella will be okay."

It took me a second to register what she'd said. "Oh! No, I'm not . . . what I mean is, Rella and I weren't exactly friends."

More like sworn enemies.

Master Sunback smiled. "I know you didn't always get along. But you were deeply connected. And it must be hard on you that she had to leave. Now, dear, is there anything else you want to talk to me about?"

I stared into Master Sunback's dark eyes. It was very hard to lie to our headmaster, and not just because she had been a teacher for more than a hundred years and knew every trick in the book. Something about her made me want to tell the truth.

But how could I? How could I admit to her that I had been looking for a shortcut with the chants too? That I wasn't any better than Rella?

Just then, Brother Chalad came jogging into the meditation garden. "You asked to see me, Master Sunback?"

She pointed to me, but I waved my hand. "It's all right, Master Sunback. I should go or I'll be late for my chores."

I bowed to both teachers and left them. On my way out of the garden, the loop of my sandal caught on the edge of a large stone. I bent to refasten it.

That's when I heard Brother Chalad say, "Did you talk to Plum?"

"No," answered Master Sunback in a hushed voice. "I didn't mention it."

Mention what?

I crouched down behind the stone and listened.

I had to strain to hear the low, scratchy sound of Master Sunback's voice. ". . . thought that surely things would have fallen into place for her by now."

"She does have some tremendous talents," said Brother Chalad. "She speaks to the vegetables in the garden and they grow even bigger. The animals in our little hospital are all thriving because when she asks them to take their medicine, they actually listen to her!"

"Hmm, that is very impressive. I've never known a Guardian who was able to do that."

Brother Chalad sighed. "But as far as healing goes, I'm

afraid she has hardly made any progress at all. She actually completed the assignment this morning, but I'm not sure if she'll be able to do it again. Is it possible that Plum isn't a Heart Guardian after all?"

"But she isn't a Hand Guardian," said Master Sunback, "and I have worked with her extensively and can detect no powers of the Breath either. It's possible that our dear Plum is her own thing entirely."

"Well, I guess that would be okay, except that . . ."

"Yes?" asked Master Sunback.

"We need all the fully trained Heart Guardians we can get."

"The lotus ponds? How are they?"

"Getting worse, I'm afraid." I could hear the worry in Brother Chalad's voice. "I heal them as fast as I can, but every morning there is more decay. It's like they are slipping away."

"Yes, they are," said Master Sunback. "The lotus plants are as ancient as the island itself. They are connected to the Guardians. As our powers fade, so too do the lotuses."

I had once overheard Master Sunback say that the Guardians' magic powers were becoming weaker, but the teachers had never said anything about this to us Novices. I didn't blame them for keeping it a secret. It was worrying to think that we were working so hard to learn powers that might be fading away.

I heard a rustle of paper. "I received another letter from Lady Ubon this morning," said Master Sunback. "She tells me again how much she wants to buy Lotus Island. Nakhon Island is growing too big, and they need more land. She points out that most of our island is unused. I can't say she is wrong."

"But then what would happen to the Guardians?" said Brother Chalad.

"I don't know. But it's hard to make the case that we need this entire island or the Academy when we are growing weaker every year."

"Surely Lady Ubon wouldn't have sent Sam, her only son, to study with us unless she thought we were important," said Brother Chalad.

"Yes, and Sam is destined to be a wonderful Guardian, I can tell," said the headmaster. "Now, back to Plum . . ."

I held my breath and listened hard.

"Perhaps her powers are just waking up very slowly. The field study on Bokati Island may be good for her."

"You think Master Em is the right Guardian to awaken her powers?" asked Brother Chalad. "He is getting a bit old."

Master Sunback chuckled. "*Getting* old? He was ancient

when I was a young Novice! But if there is one thing he knows, it's how to be surprising. Perhaps he and Plum will surprise us all. Come, Brother Chalad, I must talk to our cook about making squishy tofu for dinner . . ."

I tiptoed away and hurried into the shade of a nearby classroom before they could see me. Once they were gone, I leaned against the wall of the building.

I hated that I was doing so poorly in my training that my teachers had to discuss what to do with me.

Now I felt sure that I could never tell them about using the chants. I was already on thin ice. My only hope was that maybe my field study could break me out of this rut.

I would study hard with Master Em on Bokati Island. I would stop using my classmates' powers to complete my assignments. I wouldn't even *think* about the words of the chant!

I had to make this work.

If I didn't, the only way I could stay on Lotus Island would be as a gardener.

CHAPTER 6

Bokati Island was half a day's boat ride away, so our group departed early with Master Dew at the wheel.

"Doesn't this boat seem a little too small for such a long trip?" fretted Hetty.

Cherry clapped her hand on Hetty's shoulder. "Relax. The sea is calm today. We could even get in a couple wrestling matches. Right, Mikko?"

Salan leaned close to me and whispered, "Mikko beat Cherry in the last wrestling tournament and she's dying for a rematch."

Mikko was a Hand Guardian whose form was a big field sloth with long furry arms. His power was endurance, which was why he was the only one who could beat Cherry at wrestling. He just had to stay in the ring long enough for her to burn up all her energy.

Mikko leaned back in his seat and yawned. "No wrestling for me, thanks. This field study will be a nice vacation. No waking up at dawn. No drills. Just chilling out."

Sam smiled. "How do you know Master Em won't make us do those things?"

"He's old, isn't he?" said Mikko. "He'll go easy on us."

"I don't care about getting up early," said Hetty, winding her hair into a bun, "just as long as we get to sleep on actual beds instead of floor mats."

"Hetty, please tell us you didn't bring your satin pillow in your backpack," said Cherry.

"Just the pillowcase!" said Hetty. "And my eye mask. And maybe my slippers."

We all laughed.

She did too. "What? I like my rest time, okay? I also brought these."

She reached into her bag and pulled out a deck of cards.

"Now you're talking," said Salan. "Deal 'em out!"

I scooted closer to Hetty as she dealt the cards. She was a Breath Guardian, and her form was an indigo hare who could sense when danger was near. Even though she was much more prim and proper than I was and she could be a bit of a tattletale sometimes, I still liked her.

She had been best friends with Rella back on Nakhon Island, and she had even teamed up with Rella against me a few times. But now that Rella was out of the picture, she was much nicer to me.

That didn't mean she went easy on me in card games though.

"Read 'em and weep!" said Hetty, laying down her winning hand.

The rest of us groaned.

Sam shuffled the cards. "For the next game, I'm transforming into my wolfhund form to sniff out any cheating."

"I did *not* cheat!" said Hetty. "And no transforming, any of you. You'll make the boat too heavy and we'll all sink."

"I never got the wolfhund thing," said Cherry. "Are you a wolf? Or a hound? Which is it?"

"Oh, and what about you?" teased Sam. "Who's ever heard of a gillybear?"

"Or a field sloth," said Mikko, pointing to himself. "Are there any Guardians who transform into normal animals?"

"Nope," said Hetty. "It's part of our gift from the Great Beast. When he bestowed his powers upon the Guardians, he gave them the ability to turn into extraordinary creatures so we could protect all the 'normal' animals."

Hetty's dad was a librarian on Nakhon Island, so she knew more about the Great Beast and the Old Home than most of us.

"Hetty, the Great Beast created the Guardians a really long time ago, right?" I asked.

"Mm-hmm, that's right," she said, dealing again.

"So . . . could the power he gave us ever . . . fade away over time?"

Hetty wrinkled up her nose and laughed. "Of course not! The Great Beast was the most powerful being who ever lived. That kind of power doesn't just fade away into nothing."

I looked down at the cards in my hand. If what Hetty said was true, then what had Master Sunback and Brother Chalad been talking about?

We spent the rest of the boat ride guessing what our field study would be like. We played cards and ate snacks. Cherry and I had stuffed pomelos into everyone's backpacks, but we were saving them to have a little taste of Lotus Island while we were away.

After several hours had passed, Master Dew called out, "Novices! We're approaching Bokati Island!"

We all stood up to look. The island was blanketed in thick fog. Enormous shapes reached up through the fog toward the sky. A cold draft of air blew over us, wrapping our boat in foggy mist. I shivered and pulled my cloak out of my pack.

"Mountains?" said Cherry. "I've never climbed a mountain before. That'll be fun!"

"Maybe we'll actually get some sledding in after all," said Salan.

Master Dew zipped the boat around a few high rocks jutting out of the sea. She cut the engine and we coasted closer to the island. The fog thinned, and we burst through the mist.

I smiled. "Those aren't mountains. They're trees."

Master Dew cast the boat's anchor in the shallows near a gravel beach. We climbed over the side and sloshed through the chilly water, holding our thick cloaks up so the salt water didn't soak them.

I craned my neck to stare up at the trees that grew along the edge of the beach. Their crowns soared up out of sight, disappearing into the mist. The trunks were as big around as our lotus ponds, and they were covered with fuzzy, rust-colored bark. The mist that hung in the air dripped down our noses.

Hetty shivered and drew her cloak tighter around her shoulders. "Does the sun ever shine here?"

Cherry transformed into a gillybear and charged into the

freezing-cold water. She dove into a wave and then came back out, shaking her fur dry. "I love this! Sweat-free wrestling matches, here I come!"

Master Dew paced the beach. "Hmm, now, where is old Master Em?"

"Did you tell him what time we would be arriving?" asked Salan.

Master Dew shook her head. "The mail boat doesn't come here. If you want to tell him something, you have to talk to him face-to-face."

"Gosh, he could be anywhere," said Hetty. "How does he know we're coming at all?"

"Oh, I'm sure he knows," said Master Dew. "Master Em is a Breath Guardian, and his power is intuition."

Intuition: the ability to have gut feelings about things. Gosh, that was a cool power to have.

I walked closer to the forest. I wanted to see the Bokati trees up close.

I pressed my palms together and bowed deeply. My grandparents had taught me that ancient trees were like wise elders. They had to be treated with great respect. "It's an honor to be in your presence, Great-Grandmother," I whispered to the tree.

I listened to see if the tree would answer back. I had been

talking to plants since I was a toddler. It had been just my grandparents and me on our little island, so sometimes the plants were the only ones around I could talk to. But today this ancient tree was silent.

I reached out and placed my hand on the furry bark.

The bark shifted under my fingertips. I looked up and saw a pair of dark brown eyes staring at me.

I yelped and jumped back!

The eyes blinked, and then a face emerged from the bark. A large ape with long arms and a broad round face stepped forward from where it had been standing pressed against the tree. Its ginger-brown fur was the same color and texture as the bark of the Bokati trees.

I stumbled back toward the others as the ginger ape continued walking forward. It leaned on a staff made of bleached driftwood. The ape looked at Master Dew and grunted.

Master Dew smiled and bowed low. "It's so good to see you again, Master Em."

The ape fluttered its lips and gave a low grunt. "Knew you were coming."

CHAPTER 8

We stayed on the beach, waving to Master Dew as the boat disappeared into the mist. She would be back in a week to pick us up. I couldn't help feeling a little abandoned.

Master Em had changed out of his Guardian form. As a human, he had wide shoulders and a thick belly. A long rust-colored mustache and beard hung from his round face. We waited for instructions, but he just gave another grunt and turned to walk into the forest, tapping his staff as he went.

"I guess this means we should follow him?" whispered Sam.

I shouldered my backpack. "I don't think we have much of a choice."

We were all quiet as we followed Master Em through the tall ferns that covered the forest floor. Even Cherry was quiet . . . which for her meant asking only five questions every minute.

"What are these ferns called? Ooh, what are those? Mushrooms? Wow, this whole island is covered in trees. Really interesting. So, Master Em, have you got a nice flat place around here? Someplace to set up a wrestling mat, maybe?"

Master Em grunted.

"Do you think he actually talks or just grunts?" whispered Mikko.

Hetty cleared her throat and piped up. "Excuse me, Master Em? Will we be shown to our dorms soon? It's starting to get dark and I'm a little cold, so—"

Master Em abruptly stopped at the foot of a huge Bokati tree. "We sleep here."

He pointed up at the tree. A rope ladder hung down from somewhere high above. Master Em transformed back into his ginger ape form and began to climb. For someone so old, he was pretty fast.

Salan smiled and transformed into his Guardian form, the scissor-tailed wybird. "Race you to the top!"

Hetty rolled her eyes. "Easy for him to say. Oh, why couldn't we have gotten a normal field study assignment?"

"Well, unless we want to sleep on the ground, we've got to follow him," said Sam. "Come on."

Cherry transformed into her gillybear form and carried all our backpacks up the ladder. Sam, Hetty, and I put our hands on the rungs and started up. Mikko brought up the rear in his field sloth form.

Up and up we went until my shoulders were burning from the climb.

"Salan . . . if I fall, you'd better catch me!" I panted.

Salan swooped down beside me. "You're almost there!"

"Ugh," groaned Hetty. "That's what he said ten ladder rungs ago!"

We finally reached a stopping point and pulled our bodies onto a wide flat space formed by the first level of branches. The main trunk kept going up and out of sight.

Mikko, Cherry, and Salan transformed back into humans, and we all leaned against the branches and caught our breath.

"Where's Master Em?" asked Mikko.

Cherry starting climbing out onto one of the massive branches. "I'm having a look around!"

"Be careful!" said Hetty. "It's a long, long way down."

"Oh, wow!" Cherry called out. "You all have to see this!"

We followed the sound of her voice. One of the tree branches had a huge circular bump bulging out of its side.

"What is this thing?" asked Mikko, running his hands over the bark.

"I think it's called a burl," I said. "Trees grow them sometimes to protect themselves from insects or disease. But this is way bigger than any burl I've ever seen."

"And look!" said Cherry. "It's hollow inside!"

The lumpy growth had been carved into a round room just tall enough for Cherry to stand up in.

"I think this must be where we're sleeping!" she said.

She pointed to the three mat-covered pallets on the wood floor.

"There's another room just over there with three more pallets," said Cherry. "One for each of us!"

We set our backpacks down and flopped onto the soft mats. A paper lantern hung overhead, filling the small room with a warm glow.

"Hmm, not bad," said Hetty, bouncing lightly on her mat. "It's not a real bed, but I wouldn't expect luxury from odd Master Em."

"I think we're lucky to have beds at all," said Cherry.

"I bet all the other Novices are on bright sunny islands, having their lessons on the beach," said Hetty with a sigh.

Cherry lay back and gazed up at the ceiling. "Can you imagine living all alone out here like Master Em? It's gotta make a person a little strange."

We heard a grunt and looked up to see Master Em's wide face peering in at us.

"Come," he barked.

We gave one another an *uh-oh* look and followed after him. He led us out onto a different tree branch and into another hollowed-out room, where the boys were already waiting for us. This room was much larger, with a long table in the center.

"Sit," ordered Master Em, pointing at the empty stools.

He handed us each a wooden bowl and spoon. And then he brought out a giant pot and set it in the center of the table. Ribbons of warm steam rose from the open pot, filling the room with an herby, buttery, gingery scent.

It was the best thing I had ever smelled in my life.

Cherry breathed in deeply and licked her lips. "I told you—I *love* this Master Em guy."

We all slurped our soup noisily. Dark strands of silky seaweed floated in the creamy broth. It was so tasty and warmed me up all the way down to my toes. Master Em also served us a platter of crispy fried fern heads and roasted checkernuts. Usually on Lotus Island, we had fruit after dinner, but Master Em hadn't prepared any dessert.

"Excuse me for just a minute," I said. I hurried back to my room and grabbed one of the pomelos out of my backpack. I cracked it open and carefully peeled away the rind. I handed a bright pink segment to Master Em.

He sniffed it deeply and shut his eyes. "Ahhhh. I haven't had pomelo since I was on Lotus Island. It's been many years."

We all looked at one another. It was the most Master Em had spoken since we'd arrived.

"Master Sunback told us you used to be a teacher there," I said.

He nodded as he savored the pomelo piece. "I was her teacher, to be precise."

"Whoa, how old *are* you?" Cherry gasped.

Master Em threw his head back and laughed. "Old, little friend. The oldest thing you'll probably ever meet, aside from the Bokati trees. I was one of the first masters who restarted the Guardian Academy many, many years ago."

"Restarted?" I asked.

"Yes, there was a period of time when Lotus Island was abandoned and the wisdom of the Guardians was nearly lost. But a handful of us came back to restore what we could of the Academy. The jungle had nearly swallowed up the buildings by then! It was a lot of work, but we were able to recover much of the knowledge we had lost."

I nodded, thinking of the crumbling temple covered with vines in the forest.

"But that is old history," said Master Em. "Please, introduce yourselves."

We took turns telling him our names, what types of Guardians we were, and what powers we had.

When it was my turn, I mumbled something about being good with animals.

"Plum is being modest," said Sam. "She has an amazing way with animals *and* plants. Our garden back on Lotus Island is bursting with life because she talks to the vegetables."

Master Em raised one eyebrow. "Could you talk to the Bokati trees?"

"Well, I sort of tried it already. But usually trees this old are very quiet. It's not that they don't have anything to say, more that they don't think people are worth talking to."

"I think that is very true!" Master Em's belly shook as he laughed. "If the Bokati trees could talk, they would tell us stories of the Old Home."

We all leaned in closer to listen.

"The tale goes that when the Great Beast carried the people and animals across the sea from the Old Home, he allowed them to bring only one thing with them because they would have to hold on to him so tightly during the long journey," said Master Em. "My great-great-great-grandmother cut a rootlet of a Bokati tree. She held on to the Great Beast's mane with one hand and clutched the root in her other fist. She brought it all the way from the

Old Home and planted it here. Every Bokati tree you see is descended from that root."

Cherry clapped her hands. "Fierce woman. I love her."

Master Em turned to Sam. "You didn't introduce yourself yet, young Novice."

Sam blushed and said, "I'm a Breath Guardian, and I have powerful senses of smell and hearing when I'm in my wolfhund form. My name is Sam Ubon."

Sam nearly whispered his last name, but when Master Em heard it, he sat up straighter. "Ubon? From the noble Ubon family?"

Sam nodded shyly. His family was more powerful and wealthy than anyone else on our islands. Some of the other kids teased him for being spoiled. I knew he was embarrassed about it.

I wanted to change the subject away from Sam, so I said, "Master Em, these rooms are so interesting. Did you carve them out yourself?"

Master Em shook his head. "No, I didn't carve them. I would never, never harm the Bokati. These 'rooms' are the work of the wooly roll bugs. You'll meet them soon enough."

Salan cleared his throat. "Master Em, will you tell us what our lessons with you will be like?"

Master Em shrugged and peeled another pomelo segment. "Oh, I don't teach lessons."

Mikko grinned. "Told you," he said. "Easygoing."

But Master Em was a teacher, wasn't he? What kind of teacher didn't teach?

Master Em's eyes twinkled, but he didn't explain. "You should all get some rest. Tomorrow we start early."

Cherry slumped in her chair. "Why do all Guardian masters like to wake up early?"

Sam and I helped clear the dishes from the table. "Master Em?" I said to the old man. "I'm sorry I was so startled when I first met you. I thought you were the Bokati tree!"

"Oh, I was the tree," said Master Em, leaning on his wooden staff. "I *am* the tree. I am the wooly roll bug. I am the fern. I am the mist . . ."

Master Em continued muttering as he shuffled out of the room without saying goodbye.

When he was gone, Salan leaned across the table. "Why do I have a feeling that having *no* lessons from Master Em is actually going to be the hardest lesson we've ever had?"

There was no sunrise on Bokati Island. In the mornings, the mist just glowed lighter. Breakfast was waiting for us on the dining table: thick rice porridge with sweet beans.

After we ate, we bundled up in our wool cloaks and made our way down the Bokati trunk to the ground, where Master Em was waiting. I had to hold back a laugh when I saw him. He wore a large mushroom tucked behind his ear like a flower.

"Novices, as I told you, I do not teach lessons," said Master Em. "I have only one assignment for you. In recent weeks, my intuition has told me that I must be more vigilant than ever in my Guardian duties. My job is to protect the ancient Bokati forest at all costs. Your assignment is to help me."

He pulled the mushroom from his hair and held it out for us to see. "To do that, you must follow the knobble shroom."

Master Em handed the mushroom to Cherry. She tapped the top of it, releasing a cloud of fine golden dust. She coughed while Master Em chuckled.

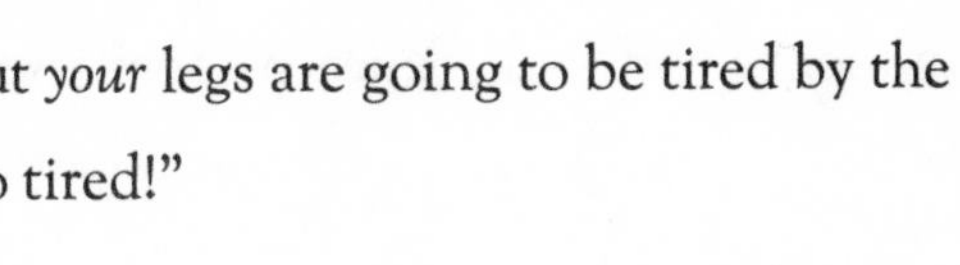

"Knobble shroom spores," he said, pointing to the dust cloud. "Tickles the throat."

"So our assignment is to follow the knobble shrooms?" asked Hetty.

Master Em nodded. "Follow them. Protect the forest."

"But, Master Em," said Salan, "how can we follow a fungus? It doesn't go anywhere."

Mikko peered under the mushroom's cap. "Maybe it has teeny-tiny legs?"

Master Em shook his head. "No legs." He laughed again, harder this time. "But *your* legs are going to be tired by the end of this. Ha-ha, so tired!"

And with that, he waddled away from us and disappeared into the mist.

"Okay," said Hetty, pointing to the mushroom. "This is obviously some sort of riddle. We just need to figure out what he means."

"Well, maybe he meant we should follow along where the knobble shrooms grow," I said. "So we just need to look for where these things are growing."

"That sounds easy," said Cherry.

But then we looked around the forest. The *very big* forest.

"I'm beginning to understand why Master Em gave us such a big breakfast," said Salan. "Where do you think we should start?"

"Well, a lot of mushrooms like to grow on decaying wood," I said. "We could look for dead trees or fallen branches."

"Good idea," said Sam. "Let's split up so we can cover more ground."

As a wybird, Salan could fly up into the trees and take a good look around. He could lead the way while Cherry and Mikko followed on the ground. In their Guardian forms, Cherry and Mikko were strong enough to lift up fallen branches and look beneath them. And Hetty, who could sense danger, would go with them to make sure no one got hurt.

Sam transformed into his wolfhund form and sniffed the knobble shroom in Cherry's hand. "I can use my senses to track down the scent." He turned to me. "Plum, you come with me, and you can . . . well, I'm sure we can figure out some way for you to be helpful!"

I sighed as I transformed into my roan form. I knew Sam wasn't trying to make me feel bad about my lack of powers, so I tried to put on a smile. "At least I'll keep you company."

CHAPTER 11

I trotted through the forest after Sam, both of us in our Guardian forms. I always liked running alongside Sam, since a roan and a wolfhund were pretty much matched in terms of speed. He swung his snout back and forth as he ran, sniffing the air.

"Smell anything yet?" I called to him.

"Just you."

"Oh, come on! And what exactly do I smell like?"

"Like pomelo rinds. And jasmine tea." Sam sniffed the air again. "And maybe like sweat that hasn't been washed away in a couple of days."

I tried to catch a whiff of myself. "Well, I guess it could be worse."

Sam slowed down. "Hold on." His black nose crinkled as he smelled the air all around us.

"Knobble shrooms?" I asked.

"Maybe." He backtracked and jogged in a wide circle. "But the scent is so faint I can't tell where it's coming from. I need three more noses to find them. Ugh, this is going to take forever."

He was right. The forest was enormous. This was never going to work.

Unless . . .

What if I used my "trick" to amplify Sam's powers, just like I had done for Salan and Cherry? But no, I had sworn to myself that I wouldn't do that again, even if our assignment depended on it.

"Plum, you've got a funny look on your face," said Sam. "What are you thinking?"

I hesitated. "If I tell you something, do you promise not to think I'm a bad person?"

"I'd never think that! What is it?"

I looked over my shoulder and lowered my voice. "So, there is this *trick* I can do. I did it with Cherry. I made her . . . well, I made her get bigger."

"Bigger? What do you mean?"

"Her powers are in her strength, right? Well, I sort of . . .

made her powers more powerful, and she became stronger and bigger. Just for a little while, and then she shrank back to normal. I did it to Salan in our last Heart class too. I increased his healing powers so we could complete our assignment." I stamped my hooves awkwardly. "I didn't tell him about it. Do you think that was wrong? Like I was cheating?"

Sam tilted his head at me. "I'm not sure. What does Master Sunback think?"

"I didn't tell her. She's already watching me because I'm not making enough progress. I didn't want to give her one more reason to worry that I don't belong at the Academy."

"Don't say that. Of course you belong with us." Sam pawed at the ground, thinking. "Did this trick of yours hurt Salan or Cherry? Or you?"

"No!" I blurted. "If it had, I would never even consider doing it again."

"Well, it does sound . . . different. But I don't think it sounds *bad*. And I'm kind of curious to know what it would be like for you to make my powers stronger."

"Are you sure?"

He nodded and placed his paw on my hoof. "Very sure. Also, I want to find these knobble shrooms before dinner."

"And you won't tell Master Em or the others?" I asked.

"Promise."

I took a deep breath and shifted closer to Sam until we stood shoulder to shoulder. I shut my eyes and imagined that Sam and I were tied together by a thin thread. It was easy to imagine—I felt as connected to Sam as I did to Cherry. My antlers started to thrum like guitar strings. I opened my eyes.

After a moment, Sam looked around. "Hmm, I don't think that worked. I don't feel any diff— Hold on." He twisted his head back and forth. "Do you hear that?"

I listened. I didn't hear anything in the muffled wetness of the forest.

"A scratching sound," said Sam. "Like tiny claws. And Plum, that smell . . ." He looked at me.

"Hey! I *will* take a shower tonight, okay?"

"Not you! I smell the knobble shrooms—*very* strongly. Come on!"

Together we galloped through the understory. Sam cut this way and that, following his nose.

Finally we arrived at the base of a Bokati tree and looked up. This one had a smaller trunk than the others in the forest. It must have been younger. Sure enough, the bumpy caps of knobble shrooms wound up the side of the trunk in a spiraling trail.

I transformed back into my human form because I just had to clap my hands. "Good work, Sam! Let's call the others!"

Soon our friends had joined us, and we all looked up at the Bokati tree, eyeing the trail of knobble shrooms.

"Look there," said Mikko, pointing to a big cluster of mushrooms about fifty feet up the trunk. The tree bark had bubbled out into a large lump, encircling the mushrooms.

"Hey, that big lump looks like a smaller version of those round rooms we sleep in," said Cherry.

Hetty ran her hand over the bark. "I think the knobble shrooms somehow make the bark grow in that strange way."

Just then we saw brown, furry things creeping down the trunk from the branches above. The creatures were about the size of piglets, and they made snorting pig sounds too. They had rounded backs and stubby antennae.

"What are those?" asked Hetty, backing closer to me.

"Oh, I know!" said Salan. "Those must be the wooly roll bugs Master Em told us about!"

The roll bugs started munching the mushrooms with their funny little mouths. I snapped my fingers. "I've got it! The knobble shrooms feed on the bark of the Bokati tree. And the tree makes this big bark bubble around the mushrooms to protect itself from getting injured."

Mikko pointed at the snorting bugs. "Then the wooly roll bugs come along and eat the knobble shrooms, hollowing out those rooms."

"So to protect the Bokati trees, just get rid of the knobble shrooms!" said Sam.

"Did we just pass the assignment?" asked Hetty with a smile.

"I think so!" said Salan. "Good work, Sam and Plum. How did you find the knobble shrooms so quickly?"

Sam tapped his nose. "I followed their scent. It wasn't easy, but Plum helped me . . . well, she helped, sort of."

"You know, Plum, you could have just made Sam's power of smell stronger," said Cherry, "like when you made me bigger that day so I could reach the pomelos."

My jaw dropped.

"What?" said Hetty, her eyes wide as knobble shroom caps.

"You *knew* I did that?" I asked Cherry.

She shrugged. "Yeah. What's the big deal? I thought it was, like, a Heart Guardian thing or something."

Salan shook his head, just as surprised as Hetty. "Definitely not a Heart Guardian thing."

Hetty folded her arms. "Plum, I think you should tell us what's going on."

I sighed. There was no point in hiding it anymore. I told them everything about my trick and how I had used it with Cherry and then with Salan.

"So *that's* why we healed all the lotuses in the pond so quickly," said Salan. "I thought something was strange that day!"

"Totally weird," said Mikko. "You're like a power booster or something."

"I'm so sorry, Salan," I said. "Please don't be mad at me. And please don't say anything to any of our teachers. I'm already worried that they don't know what to do with me."

Just then we heard the slow tapping of Master Em's staff coming toward us. "How is your work going, Novices?"

"*Don't say anything,*" I mouthed to the others.

They all nodded.

We rushed to tell him what we had discovered and that we had completed his assignment and passed our test. But when we were done talking, he just shook his head at us. "Nope. The knobble shrooms are important. Getting rid of them would be a very bad idea."

"But they eat the bark," said Salan.

"You told us to figure out how to protect the Bokati trees," said Hetty. "That's what we did."

"I told you to follow the knobble shrooms," said Master Em.

"We did, Master Em. We—"

"You didn't follow them *all the way*."

Master Em pointed up the trunk of the Bokati tree. We looked at the spot where the wooly roll bugs were still feasting on the knobble shroom patch.

One of the roll bugs stuck out its round bottom and released a stream of dark brown spheres that fell to the ground with a soft *plop!*

Master Em pointed at the steaming brown pile. "Follow the knobble shrooms."

Hetty whimpered.

Cherry wrinkled her nose. "Master Em, when you said follow them, we didn't think you meant follow them through the digestive tract."

But Master Em had already started walking away.

I sighed and looked at Sam.

He held up his hands and shook his head. "Nope. No way. I will use my sense of smell to help us, but I draw the line at roll bug poop!"

CHAPTER 12

We stood there, staring at the poop.

It wasn't going anywhere. Not by itself, anyway.

Salan yawned. "How long do you think we have to do this?"

Cherry pointed at the ground. "Hey, look—something's happening!"

Spindly insects started to come out of the leaf litter. "I think those are called dung-hoppers," I said.

One by one, the dung-hoppers nudged the balls of wooly roll bug poop away from the piles and began rolling them across the ground. We followed them, hunched over, shuffling along. The beetle dung smelled kind of like wet hay.

"What do you think the other Novices would say if they could see us now?" asked Mikko.

"We are never *ever* telling anyone back on Lotus Island about this!" said Hetty.

The dung-hoppers rolled the balls to tunnels they had dug beneath the Bokati tree roots. As the dung-hoppers worked on getting the poop into their tunnels, screeching green mosskeets swooped down from the branches overhead and plucked up the insects with their beaks.

We all looked at one another.

"Follow the mosskeets?" I offered.

So we tracked the lime-green birds through the forest all the way to the edge of the island, where they nested. Their nests were made of big piles of moss and twigs built on Bokati branches that hung way out over the water.

We watched the adult birds feed the dung-hoppers to their babies. The fuzzy little fledglings hopped about in the nests. Every now and then, they released dribbles of white droppings into the shallow water below.

"Not more poop!" whined Hetty.

"Well, how do we follow *that*?" asked Mikko.

Sam pointed at the far end of the beach, where a raft made of Bokati driftwood bobbed in the shallows, tied to a boulder.

“That should hold us, don’t you think?”

“But we haven’t got any oars,” said Salan.

Cherry transformed into her gillybear form and plunged into the cool water. “Perfect timing—I was dying for a swim!”

“In the poo water?” called Salan.

Cherry splashed water at all of us. “It’s the ocean—there’s always a little poo in it! Come on!”

We climbed aboard the raft and Cherry pushed us along with her nose. Even though the raft was bleached and faded, it floated high above the water and kept us perfectly dry. Cherry kept us in the shallows, where the water was crystal clear. The mosskeet nests were directly above us.

Hetty covered her head with her arms. “If I get mosskeet poop in my hair, I’ll never speak to any of you again.”

Salan pointed down at the water. “The mosskeet droppings must fertilize those kelp beds.”

“I’ll check it out!” Cherry ducked under the water, then surfaced again.

“I wish you could see this!” she said. “There are all these teeny-tiny shrimp that live in the kelp. And there are big pink blushfish hunting them.”

“Follow the blushfish!” we cried out as one.

Cherry dove underwater again, startling the fish. They made a rosy swirl on the surface as they swam away.

Cherry nudged our raft through the water along the rocky shore until we reached the mouth of a small river that dumped into the ocean.

Cherry popped her head up to tell us, "The blushfish are headed up the river!"

"If we are going to follow the knobble shrooms, we've got to follow the fish!" said Sam.

Cherry pushed our raft against the current until the river choked down into a trickling stream. When the raft started to drag along the rocks at the bottom, Cherry stood up and shook out her fur, spraying us all with icy water.

"Hey! If I wanted a shower, I'd take one!" said Mikko.

Sam laughed. "Actually, you *could* use a shower."

Sleek brown ottums dove in and out of the stream. They looked at us with big black eyes peeking out of furry round faces. With a twitch of their whiskers, they returned to catching the blushfish and dragging them up onto the mossy banks of the river. The ottums feasted on the fish and left the scales and bones among the roots of the Bokati trees.

Suddenly it all clicked for us.

"The knobble shrooms feed on the Bokati bark . . ."

"The wooly roll bugs eat the knobble shrooms . . ."

"Their dung is gathered by the dung-hoppers, which are eaten by mosskeets . . ."

"Whose droppings help the kelp grow, where blushfish feed on tiny shrimp . . ."

"The blushfish swim upstream, where they are hunted by the ottums . . ."

"And their remains provide nutrients for the Bokati trees!" cried Cherry.

"And then it all starts again," I said.

"Whoa, my head is about to explode!" said Salan.

I looked up at the mist hanging in the air. The Bokati trees were so big. Could they be big enough to create their own weather? And who knew what connections there were between this island and the other islands of our archipelago.

"So that means that if we want to protect the Bokati trees . . ." said Hetty.

"We have to take care of it all," I said. "It's all connected."

"So does this mean we actually completed the assignment this time?" asked Sam.

"Let's go find Master Em and tell him!"

We started to race through the forest toward Master Em's tree. As we ran, I noticed something strange out of the corner of my eye. I slowed down.

"Plum? What is it?" called Cherry.

"That doesn't seem right," I said, backtracking.

Through the trees, I saw . . . emptiness.

I wasn't a Breath Guardian with the power of intuition like Master Em. But I knew instantly that something was wrong.

I crept closer. The mist thinned and a jagged scrap of sky opened overhead. There was nothing—no Bokati trees, no ferns, no mosskeets.

Straight ahead, we saw the massive stump of a Bokati tree. The top of it was sawn clean off as if someone had sliced through it with a sharp blade.

My heart dropped as the others ran to join me.

"Oh no!" Hetty gasped. "We have to find Master Em."

CHAPTER 13

Master Em knelt next to the Bokati stump and ran his hand back and forth over the smooth cut. He was quiet for a long time before saying in a hoarse voice, "I had a feeling something bad would happen soon, but I never could have predicted this. The cut is at least a few days old. The sap has already hardened."

Hetty had transformed into her Guardian form, the indigo hare. She rotated her long ears back and forth. "I don't sense any danger . . . none at all. Whoever—or *whatever*—did this, they're gone now."

Salan knelt beside Master Em and placed his hands on the ruined stump. "I don't think I could heal it even if I were the most powerful Heart Guardian in the world."

I knew that even if I boosted Salan's powers, it still wouldn't be enough. I paced back and forth. I felt so angry, so frustrated that there was nothing I could do.

Master Em rose to his feet and leaned on his staff. "I always knew that one day the Bokati trees would come under threat. Their wood is more valuable than gold. Just one Bokati tree has enough timber to make an entire ship."

I thought of the driftwood raft we had ridden. It had floated so well. If you had a boat made of the same wood, it would be unsinkable.

"Master Em," said Sam, "who do you think did this?"

He shook his head. "I have no idea. Only someone who denies all that is sacred in this world would have the heart to take one of these ancient trees."

"I'll write a message to my mother," said Sam. "She will make sure that whoever is responsible is brought to justice."

"And we should tell Master Sunback!" said Mikko. "She should know about this!"

Master Em nodded. "I will send her a message as soon as I can. But it will be several days before the boat from Lotus Island returns, and there is no way to get a message out sooner."

We all looked at one another. I could tell my friends felt like I did—all alone at the end of the world.

"Tonight I will light a candle for this tree," said Master Em. "I will sit in memory of all it lived through. A being such as this deserves to be honored."

"I'll sit with you," I said.

"And me," said Cherry.

The others nodded. We would all stay with Master Em.

He gave us a slight smile as he turned. "Come. We will gather incense and offerings for the sitting."

As I walked with him, he cast a look back at the tree.

"What is it, Master Em?" I asked him.

"I sense that this is not over, Plum."

I frowned as I followed the others through the forest. This was not some simple assignment. This was real life.

CHAPTER 14

As the forest darkened, we set up a small altar near the tree stump. We lit candles and incense. And we set out what nice things we had for the spirit of the tree: pomelo segments and cups of sweet tea that Master Em brewed from fennel roots. I sat on my knees with the others and shut my eyes, my hands pressed together in front of me.

"Oh, Great-Grandmother Bokati," I whispered. "We are so sorry this happened to you. Wherever your spirit may be, we hope it is at peace."

The flickering candles and our lanterns cast wavering shadows through the forest. I sat in stillness for a long time. And then, strangely, I thought I could hear the voice of the Bokati tree speaking back to me.

So sad . . . so, so sad and foolish.

My eyes popped open. Yes, the words I had heard had clearly come from the Bokati. But how? There was no more tree to do the speaking.

"Master Em?" I said. "This may sound strange, but I can feel that this Bokati tree has something to say."

Master Em looked at me curiously. "Hmm, maybe you feel the tree's spirit. But she is gone."

I nodded, keeping my thoughts to myself. I had the strangest feeling that she *wasn't* gone. The tree was hurt, but she was still here somehow.

Suddenly Hetty stood up. She had a funny look on her face. She transformed into her indigo hare form. Her long ears flicked this way, then that.

"Uh-oh," said Cherry. "I don't like it when Hetty gets like this."

"Are we in danger, Hetty?" asked Master Em.

Hetty thumped her foot in frustration. "I can't tell. Maybe if Plum does her power trick on me, I'll be able to."

The other Novices gasped.

"Hetty, you tattletale!" said Cherry with a scowl.

Master Em raised his eyebrows. "*What* power trick?"

I bit my lip. I should have known Hetty would never be

able to keep a secret. "I can increase the powers of the other Novices," I said quietly. "For a short while, anyway."

Master Em looked at me strangely. Was he angry? Disappointed?

"Please, I can explain—" I started to say.

He pointed from me to Hetty. "If this is true, you must do it now. If we're all in danger, we need to know where it's coming from."

I nodded and transformed into the roan. Hetty placed her paw on my hoof, and I shut my eyes to do my trick. My antlers tingled and I felt that faint thread between Hetty and me.

Hetty gasped. "It's here! Whatever came here before is back!"

We all huddled close together.

"Are *we* in danger, Hetty?" asked Master Em.

She shut her eyes and twitched her ears. "No. Whatever it is, it's here for the trees."

The tingling in my antlers faded, and Hetty opened her eyes. "That's all I can sense."

"We must try to stop them," said Master Em.

Sam transformed into his wolfhund form and pricked up his ears. "I hear something. It's coming from this way!"

We followed Sam through the forest, Master Em holding his lantern high to light the way.

"I hear a buzzing sound, like mosquitoes," said Sam.

He was right. After a while, we got close enough that even I could hear it.

As we walked on, a thick fog crept in around us. This fog was different from the usual mist—it was thick and as dark as the night itself.

"Everyone be still!" called Master Em.

The fog grew denser, choking out the lantern light and throwing us into darkness.

I turned this way and that. "Sam? Cherry? Master Em!"

The others called out. I could hear them, but I couldn't see anyone. I was wound up in a shadow like a fly caught in a web. The high-pitched buzz grew louder and louder.

"Plum! Plum!" called Cherry. "Where are you?"

"Plum!" Sam's voice sounded faint and far away.

My throat tightened. What if my friends were in trouble? I planted my hooves on the ground. I shut my eyes tight and focused on the vision of finding them. I felt heat encircle me, like the warmth of a fire.

I opened my eyes, hardly believing what I saw. The fog was lit up with a ruby-red light. My antlers were glowing like a torch.

"There! I see you, Plum!" called Cherry. A moment later, she pierced through the fog and ran to me.

The others followed. We huddled together, everyone placing a hand on my back.

"Stay close to Plum, everyone!" called Master Em.

The buzzing grew louder and louder. Hetty covered her ears and shut her eyes. All four of my legs were shaking. I had never felt so frightened.

And then, just as suddenly as it had started, the buzzing stopped. For a brief moment, the only thing I could hear was the ringing in my ears. And then we heard the loud sounds of branches cracking and leaves swishing. The sounds floated up and away from us, like they were soaring up, up into the sky.

Then the forest went silent.

The glow from my antlers faded. Master Em held his lantern high. The shadowy mist thinned, and the silhouettes of the trees became visible again.

We walked around slowly, in a daze.

We all seemed to be okay. No one was hurt.

But then I heard Mikko exclaim, "Oh no!"

We rushed to his side. A breeze blew through the woods, sweeping away the last shreds of fog.

Another Bokati tree, this one even bigger than the last, was gone. All that remained was the stump, dripping with fresh sap.

CHAPTER 15

We sat at the table in Master Em's great room while he paced back and forth.

I still felt stunned. "What just happened?" I asked.

"I feel like I can still hear that awful buzzing sound in my brain," said Sam.

"What about that roaring rush of wind?" asked Salan. "And then the tree was just *gone*. Like it had been plucked up into the sky!"

"Do you think it was some sort of tornado?" asked Hetty.

Mikko raised an eyebrow. "A tornado that destroyed just one tree? Come on."

"You don't know!" said Hetty. "No one could see anything with that shadow mist all around us!"

"That cut was way too clean to have been a tornado," said Cherry. "That cut was made by a blade."

Suddenly Master Em roared, "This is an all-out attack!" He slammed his fist down on the table, and we all held on to our teacups so they wouldn't topple over. "Someone thinks they can just come to this island and take the trees!"

"It's monstrous," said Hetty. "I can't believe it."

"One tree was bad enough, but two?" said Salan.

"It could be more than two," said Mikko.

Master Em stomped even harder, and we all had to hold on to our teacups to keep them from falling over. I gave Mikko a look.

"What?" he said, shrugging. "You know you were thinking the same thing."

Master Em suddenly turned to me. "Plum. The thing you did with Hetty—your trick. You've done that before?"

I looked at Cherry, then at Sam. They both looked away.

Great. Thanks, guys. Guess I'm on my own here.

I gulped. "Yes. The first time was back on Lotus Island. I made Cherry grow bigger and stronger so she could pick pomelos that were growing high up."

Cherry held up one of the pomelo fruits. "Remember how much you liked these, Master Em?"

He pushed it out of the way and narrowed his eyes at

me. "I have never heard of a Guardian being able to make another Guardian's powers stronger."

I looked down at the table. "Yeah, well, apparently I'm kind of weird when it comes to being a Guardian."

"Don't be mad at Plum," said Sam. "Without her, I never would have been able to find those knobble shrooms."

I smacked my palm against my forehead.

"Um, not that we were cheating!" added Sam quickly.

"Enough!" said Master Em. He pointed a finger at me. "You."

I gulped again.

Then Master Em unclenched his fist and held up his palm. "I want you to use your trick to magnify my powers."

"You mean your powers of intuition?" I squeaked. "Master Em, I don't know if I can do that."

Master Em slumped into the seat next to me. "Please, Plum. I have to know what will happen to the Bokati. I have to try to see their future."

I looked up at Master Em. His eyes were so dark they were nearly black. "Okay. I'll do my best."

The others pushed their chairs out of the way so I would have room to transform into the roan. Master Em transformed into his ginger ape form and placed his long leathery fingers on my forehead.

We both shut our eyes, and I began.

I started the same way as I had with my friends: trying to imagine that thin, invisible strand connecting us. But with Master Em, I couldn't picture it. I took another breath and focused on the weight of his hand on my forehead.

Master Em didn't make me think of a whisper-thin silk strand. He made me think of a tree root that grew deep, deep in the ground. And when I thought of being connected to him, I thought about walking on the earth and knowing the roots were beneath my feet.

Zing!

There was the feeling in my antlers. Master Em must have felt it too, because he pulled his hand away from me like I had shocked him.

I opened my eyes. Master Em kept his shut. His face twisted this way and that, like he was having a strange waking dream.

We all held very still and quiet, and after a long time, he opened his eyes.

"Master Em, what did you see?" I whispered.

His voice was so quiet we almost couldn't hear him. "Gone. All gone. I see a world without Bokati trees. They are all gone."

Hetty covered her mouth. Sam hung his head.

Strangely, Master Em broke into a wide smile. And then he opened his eyes and laughed. We all looked at one another. What did this mean?

"I saw a world in which all the Bokati trees were gone," said Master Em. "But the truth is that *everything* will be gone one day. The Bokati trees, me, you. Nothing in this world lasts forever." He chuckled to himself again. "Plum, this has been a lesson to not take my powers so seriously."

"So I guess my trick wasn't so helpful?"

Master Em grew serious again. "No, Plum, it was most helpful, actually. Because it was a reminder to me that one day everything will be gone, but how it will go has not been determined. It could be tomorrow. It could be ten thousand years from now. Even so, I am not powerless. I have a say in how it all unfolds. The Bokati need a defender. I will fight for them as long as I can."

Cherry stood up and placed her hands on the table. "I will too!"

Sam stood up. "And me. Whoever this person is, they can't come in here and take the Bokati trees!"

"It's not just the trees," said Salan. "Think of the wooly roll bugs, the mosskeets, the ottums. Everything depends on the Bokati. All of them will disappear if we don't save the trees."

"Think of the poop!" said Hetty.

"We're not leaving, Master Em," said Mikko. "We're helping you in this fight."

Master Em's smile returned, wider than before. "You know what? I had a feeling you would say that."

CHAPTER 16

The next morning, Master Em gathered us after a quick breakfast. "We must determine where the next attack will happen. We cannot be caught off guard again."

Master Em drew us a map of the island, which he knew by heart. He gave the map to Salan and sent him out to do some scouting. It took him until lunch to fly over most of the island. Sadly he found that even more Bokati trees had been taken than we'd thought.

"*Three* more trees?" I asked when he returned. "Are you sure?"

Salan nodded gravely. "Definitely sure. The cuts looked even older than on that first tree we found. Someone has been quietly harvesting Bokati trees for at least a couple of weeks."

We all bowed our heads. But Master Em would not let us feel defeated. "Hetty, did you mark on the map where the missing trees are?"

She nodded and held the map out for us. "It's strange—the targets are all in a wide circle, always near the shoreline. And they're spaced out evenly, kind of like a pattern."

"Why do you think the thieves are spacing out the attacks?" asked Sam.

"So they won't get caught, obviously," said Mikko. "And they probably pick trees close to the shore so they can get to their targets without anyone catching them."

Cherry pounded her fist into her palm. "Well, we are catching them this time!"

I pointed at the map. "Based on this, if the attackers stick to this pattern, we can assume the next tree targeted will be somewhere around here."

"And I think we can guess the attack will happen at night again," said Salan.

"Yes, when that shadow mist makes it hard to see."

Master Em rubbed his beard. "Our next task is to understand our attackers. We cannot fight this . . . *thing* if we don't even know what it is."

Cherry nodded. "It's like Master Dew always says: *Know your opponent. Their weakness is your strength.*"

Master Em smiled. "Exactly. To do that, we must all join together. Plum, we are going to need to put your weirdness to work."

That afternoon, I practiced using my trick on my friends.

With a boost from me, Mikko had so much endurance that he could climb to the top of a Bokati tree and back down without even breaking a sweat. With my help, Sam could hear the footsteps of ants in their tunnels beneath the ground. And I made Cherry so strong that she could pick up Mikko (in his giant field sloth form) and hold him off the ground!

The more I did it, the less I had to imagine something like a silk thread or a tree root. Pretty soon, all I had to do was shut my eyes, and I would instantly feel that surge of connection between the other Novice and me. It was all starting to click.

Their boosted powers still faded away after a little while, and afterward I felt tired and needed to sit down and rest. But each time we did it, my friends' powers grew stronger and lasted longer than before.

"All right, I think we need to give Plum a break now," said Master Em. "Mikko, we need to help you work on the tools we will use tonight."

Mikko nodded. "I already have the design sketched up. If the rest of you help me gather materials, they won't take long to make."

"Excellent," said Master Em. "We will go with you to help. Hetty, you stay here with Plum and make sure she takes a nice long rest."

As the others walked away, Hetty and I plopped down together in a lush patch of ferns.

"You did some great work today," said Hetty.

"Thanks! It's so cool to watch all of your powers get even more amazing with my trick."

"Can I tell you something?" said Hetty. "I don't think you should call this thing your 'trick' anymore. I think the ability to boost everyone else's power is *your* power."

"But it's not typical—"

"Who cares?" said Hetty. "It's incredible. And without it, we'd have no chance of protecting the Bokati trees."

I smiled. "Thank you. Now can I tell *you* something?"

"Uh-oh. Okay, fire away."

"I like you better than I did before," I said.

Hetty thought for a moment, then nodded. "You mean without Rella. Yeah, I think I like me better too."

"Why were you even friends with her? She was so mean!"

"You may not believe this," said Hetty, "but Rella could

be a good friend sometimes. Back on Nakhon Island, she knew I was alone a lot because my dad was working at the library all the time. She always stayed with me after school so I wouldn't be lonely. And she always gave me little presents on holidays even though she didn't have a lot of money."

"Rella? Not have money?" I asked. "She was always so perfectly dressed. And she made fun of me for being a farm girl with dirty fingernails!"

Hetty nodded. "There's a lot she hides. She hasn't had it easy. That's no excuse for being mean to you, but it might help you understand why she is the way she is."

Hetty took a deep breath and looked around. The light shining through the misty air hit the ferns just right, making them glow like jade.

"I never thought I'd say this," said Hetty, "but Bokati Island is really beautiful."

I smiled. "I think so too."

I looked up into the tree branches high overhead. This was maybe the most peaceful place I had ever been.

I just hoped we could save it.

CHAPTER 17

That evening, before darkness settled on Bokati Island, we gathered in the area where we predicted the next attack would be. We were all nervous.

If we hadn't had Master Em to give us guidance, we probably would have spent those last few minutes before dusk pacing back and forth, listening to Cherry talk up a storm.

Instead we all sat on the ground and closed our eyes to meditate. We breathed in and out, focusing on our breath and our bodies so our minds would stop running away from us. After a few minutes, I felt my heart beat more slowly. My breath came more steadily. There was something else too.

When I was quiet, and when my mind was quiet, I could

focus on listening to the sounds of the forest. I heard the roll bugs.

Munch, munch, we munch the knobble shrooms.

I heard the mosskeets.

Night is coming! Back to the nests! To the babies!

And then—very faintly—I heard the sound of the Bokati trees.

Coming. They are coming back.

My eyes popped open.

"Hetty," I whispered. "I think we need you now."

Without another word, Hetty and I both transformed. She placed her paw on my foreleg.

Her dark blue coat shivered all over and her nose twitched. "It's back. And it's coming closer."

"Sam, you're up next," said Master Em.

Sam transformed into the wolfhund so I could boost his powers. His ears pricked up. "I hear the buzzing! It's this way!"

We followed him until we could all hear the buzzing. Soon it was as loud as being in the center of a beehive. But as we closed in, the shadow mist encircled us. We couldn't see a thing.

"Stay together this time," advised Master Em.

The rest of the group transformed into their Guardian forms, and we all stood backed up against one another.

"Mikko," said Master Em, "we need you now!"

Mikko turned to me and placed his sloth paw on my flank.

When he opened his eyes, he picked up two enormous fans. He had spent all afternoon making them from pieces of Bokati bark. Mikko furiously began waving the fans through the air, creating a strong gust of wind. The shadow mist started to swirl away from us.

"It's working," said Salan. "Faster, Mikko!"

Mikko waved the fans at double speed. With the boost from me, he had even more endurance than normal. But still, he was working so hard. I wondered how long he could keep it up. The shadow mist refused to clear completely.

With a roar, Mikko gave one last burst with the fans. His efforts pushed the mist back for one brief moment.

I gasped. "Can that *be*?"

Hoverbots. At least twenty, maybe thirty, surrounded the base of an enormous Bokati tree.

"No, that's impossible," whispered Sam.

The high-pitched buzzing sounds came from saws that jutted out of their bodies. Sawdust sprayed into the air as they dug their saws into the soft bark of the tree.

Cherry tapped my shoulder with her gillybear claws. "Plum, you better give me a boost."

"Look at their saws," I said. "It's too dangerous!"

"Plum—"

"Cherry, I can't!"

"For the love of pomelos, you'd better DO IT!"

She clamped her paw onto my shoulder, and I shut my eyes.

Cherry grew. And grew. And grew.

Then she threw back her massive head and growled as she bared her razor-sharp teeth.

And she charged into the throng.

CHAPTER 18

Everything that happened next was a blur. Cherry rushed toward one of the hoverbots, claws out. She swatted the bot away from the Bokati tree. The bot spun out of control and slammed into the ground.

My heart squeezed tight as I watched my best friend put herself in such danger. The hoverbots had those sharp saws. What if they all turned and attacked Cherry? But they didn't even seem to notice her. They stayed focused on cutting into the tree.

Mikko dropped his fans. He rushed to Cherry's side and grabbed a hoverbot. He slung it away from the tree so hard that it slammed into another bot with a loud crash. Metal parts flew through the air in all directions.

"Come on, let's help them!" called Sam.

We all jumped into the fight. The trick was to use the hoverbots' spinning motion against them. If one bot got spun off its axis, it would lose control and crash into the ground or into other bots. As long as we stayed away from their saw blades, they couldn't hurt us.

In my roan form, I galloped straight for a hoverbot and butted it with my forehead. It went whizzing away from the tree and ground into the dirt like a drill.

"Yes, Plum!" Cherry pumped her fist at me before diving back into the fight beside Hetty and Salan. Even Master Em swung his staff this way and that, whacking the hoverbots and knocking them off balance.

I smiled to myself. Master Dew would be so proud of the way we were using the bots' own momentum against them.

But then, just as quickly as it had lifted, the shadow mist returned. It covered everything, and we couldn't see more than a foot in front of us. We couldn't see the bots at all.

"Cherry, take this!" called Master Em. He pressed his staff into her paws.

Cherry swung the staff through the mist. I couldn't see her, but I could hear the whiz of the staff and the metallic clang of the wood making contact with a hoverbot.

Through the sounds of crunching metal and crashing

bots, I heard someone whistle, and then a voice spoke three short words.

I froze.

I recognized that voice. And I recognized those words.

They were words from the chants painted on the temple walls on Lotus Island.

The mosquito buzzing stopped. The shadow mist drifted away from the Bokati tree and began retreating through the forest, toward the shore.

"What's happening?" asked Hetty.

"The mist is leaving. The hoverbots must be running away!"

The others cheered, but I didn't join them. I put my head down and galloped after the mist.

"Plum! Where are you going?"

I sprinted behind the retreating mist. It swirled away from me like smoke through the trees, faster and faster. Every now and then I caught a glimpse of a hoverbot hidden in the cloud of mist.

I forced my legs to go faster. I would not lose them.

Finally the mist reached the shore of the island. I hung back behind the tree line, gasping to catch my breath.

The beach was bathed in pale moonlight that reflected off the water. I watched as the mist gathered into a ball that shrank smaller and smaller. The remaining hoverbots left the shore and sped away across the water, toward the dark horizon.

One last hoverbot waited on the shore. It retracted its saw blades and lowered a platform from a panel in its back. A figure stepped out of the disappearing mist.

It was a large gray leopard. With a shake of its smoke-gray coat, the leopard shifted into its human form.

The person climbed onto the hoverbot's platform, holding on to the top of the bot to keep steady. And then the bot took off, spraying seawater in its wake.

I watched them zip across the water.

"I should have known," I whispered to myself. "Rella."

When I returned to the others, they were standing around the trunk of the Bokati tree in their human forms, surveying the wreckage of metal and hoverbot parts.

Cherry pointed to what was left of a destroyed bot. She pumped both arms in the air. "That was *awesome*! We totally defeated those bots!"

"We sure did," said Mikko, giving her a high five. "I wish Master Dew could have seen us. Hetty, even you were charging in there!"

Hetty bowed with a flourish. "Why, thank you. I consider myself a true bot destroyer now."

They all laughed as they recounted how great the battle had been. But I wasn't in a cheerful mood. I knew what the hoverbots meant. Hoverbots had been invented on Nakhon Island by Sam's mom, Lady Ubon.

I looked around for Sam. I spotted him sitting apart from the others, crouching over the remnants of a hoverbot.

"Sam?" I asked as I jogged up to him. "Are you okay?"

"I just don't understand," he said quietly. "The hoverbots of Nakhon Island were designed to help humans, to make our lives better. They don't attack. They don't destroy. My mother would never— She'd be horrified to know her creations were doing this! There has to be some logical explanation."

My mind was spinning, also trying to come up with an explanation. I remembered that on the day Rella had left Lotus Island, she had received an invitation to go to work for Lady Ubon. And now she had shown up here with Lady Ubon's hoverbots.

"The hoverbots must have some kind of glitch," said Sam. "Maybe something went wrong with their programming."

"I don't think it's a glitch," I said. "I followed the hover-bots to the shore. Rella was with them."

Sam looked shocked. "Rella!"

I nodded. "I should have guessed it was her. She showed me her Guardian powers once on Lotus Island. She could create shadows. But her powers have gotten so much stronger now."

"But what would Rella be doing here?" asked Sam.

"I never told you this, but after she left the Guardian Academy, she went back to Nakhon Island . . . to work for your mother."

Sam shot to his feet. "What are you saying, Plum? That my mother had something to do with this?"

The others jogged over to see what we were arguing about.

"Sam, please don't be upset," I said to him. "All I'm saying is—"

Sam twisted away from me. "I can't believe you, Plum. I thought you were my friend. I never thought you'd accuse my family of something so terrible. You're just like everyone else!"

His eyes filled with tears and he took off running.

"Sam, wait!" I started after him, but Master Em held my arm.

"Let him go for now," said Master Em. "Sam needs to be alone."

Behind us we heard Salan call out, "Plum! Master Em! Come here!"

We ran back to the Bokati tree, where Salan knelt. He held both his hands over a deep gash in the trunk. Clear sap oozed out of the cut and onto his fingers.

"The hoverbots made a deeper cut than we realized," said Salan. He transformed into his wybird form and pressed his wings against the gash. "Help me, Plum?"

I nodded. I transformed into the roan and connected with Salan. He beat his wings over the gash, slow and steady. The tree bark knitted over itself and fused back together. There was a dark deep scar where the tree had been cut, but it would be all right.

I transformed back into my human form and sat on the ground heavily.

"Plum? Are you okay?" asked Cherry.

"Just tired," I said. "I think it's because I used this trick—"

Hetty cleared her throat.

"—used this *power* so many times in one day."

"You were great, Plum," said Salan. "At least we saved this tree."

I placed my hand against the tree's trunk and whispered, "Wise old Bokati, you are healed."

But I felt something strange. It was like I could hear the Bokati whispering back to me.

No, not safe. Hurt. Still hurt.

I leaned in closer to the tree. "You are still hurt? Is that what you said?"

When one is cut, we share the pain. We can lose no more.

Suddenly I had a realization.

"Master Em," I said. "You told us your ancestor brought a Bokati root from the Old Home. How do new Bokati trees grow? Do they have seeds?"

Master Em shook his head. "No, they don't grow from seeds. New trees grow from the roots of old ones."

"So all the trees in the forest are really just one big tree?" asked Cherry.

He nodded slowly. "I suppose you could say that. All the trees in the forest grew from that first tree long ago."

"Master Em, I think we saved this one tree, but it still feels the painful loss of the others."

"That means when one tree is cut down . . ." said Hetty.

". . . all the other trees feel it," said Mikko.

Master Em frowned. "This means that if we continue to lose trees, the entire forest could be damaged." He looked at me. "Plum, can you hear the Bokati? Are they suffering?"

"Yes," I said. "I don't think we can lose even one more."

"And what if we are attacked again?" he asked.

"Then we'll fight again!" said Cherry. But even energetic Cherry sounded tired.

"We barely saved this one tree. And we got lucky," said Mikko. "I don't think I can do this every night."

"There's something else you should know," I said. "The shadow mist is being created by Rella."

"*Rella!*" they all gasped as one.

I told them how I had followed the mist and seen Rella on the shore. Master Em didn't know who she was, so I gave him the short version of Rella's story and explained why she'd had to leave Lotus Island.

"She seems much more powerful than the last time I saw her," I told them.

"Too bad she turned out like this," said Mikko, shaking his head sadly. "She was the best Novice in our Hand class."

Master Em looked puzzled. "A Hand Guardian? But the power to create shadows is a Breath Guardian trait."

Cherry snorted. "Breath Guardian! No way. She never went to a single Breath class. That girl was always making trouble."

"But what is she doing here?" asked Salan.

"Yeah, and how could she carry away a whole Bokati tree by herself?" asked Mikko.

"But she *wasn't* by herself," said Hetty. "Those hoverbots are very strong, and she had at least thirty of them."

I explained that Rella had started working for Lady Ubon after she'd left Lotus Island. I felt guilty for connecting

Sam's mom to the attack, but there could be no more secrets between any of us.

"Maybe Rella stole Lady Ubon's hoverbots to cut down the trees," said Salan. "And then the bots lifted the trees up and carried them back to Nakhon Island."

"Master Em, you told us the wood is very valuable," said Mikko. "She must want it for something."

Master Em smoothed down his long beard, thinking. "This is all very strange. Yes, the Bokati wood is valuable. But what would a young girl like Rella do with so much of it? It doesn't make sense."

"Knowing Rella, she wouldn't do something like this without a reason," said Hetty. "I know she can be mean, but she's not the type of person who would cut down trees just to be cruel. And there's something else I know about her." Hetty looked at each of us. "When she wants something, she won't stop until she gets it. She didn't get this tree. But I think she'll be back for another one."

The morning sun began to light up the forest. Master Em held up his hands. "Novices, we will make a plan to address this new information. But for now we must rest so that we can think clearly."

"What about Sam?" I asked.

"Sam will come back when he's ready," said Master Em. "He knows how to find us."

Even Cherry was silent as we trudged wearily through the forest to Master Em's house. I had a feeling we were all thinking the same thing.

How do you stop a shadow?

I opened my eyes, confused that it was so bright outside. It seemed like midafternoon, but I felt like I had just gone to sleep a few seconds ago. I sat up and looked around our room. Cherry and Hetty slept heavily on their mats. I stood up and wrapped myself in my cloak.

Salan and Mikko lay on their mats in the next room, curled up like roll bugs. There was still no sign of Sam. I tiptoed into the dining room, but no one was there.

I climbed down to the ground, hoping to see Sam walking up any moment. Instead, I found Master Em, sitting with his back against the tree trunk. His legs were folded beneath him, and his eyes were closed. I sat nearby and shut my eyes too.

Not long ago, I would not have wanted to meditate at a time like this. I would have wanted to talk and think and think and think about my problems. But Master Sunback had taught me that holding tight to my problems didn't make them any smaller.

It took me a while to get settled, but I listened to the sound of my breath and the sound of Master Em's breath.

My breath goes in. My breath goes out. Master Em's breath goes in. It goes back out.

After a while of doing this, I opened my eyes. A few seconds later, Master Em opened his eyes and smiled at me.

I realized that even though we were facing a huge problem with Rella and the hoverbots, I couldn't help solve it until I addressed another problem.

My secret about using the chants was like a thorn in the bottom of my foot. I had to get it out, even if it meant I would be in trouble. Even if it meant I would have to leave the Guardian Academy, I couldn't keep the secret inside anymore.

"Master Em, I need to tell you something . . ."

I told him everything about the temple ruins and the chants. I told him how Rella had used them as a shortcut to transform and how the chants had given her the power to create the shadow mist. I also confessed to speaking the chants myself.

"Ah, the chants written on the temple walls," said Master Em.

"You know them?"

He nodded. "We discovered them many, many years ago, when I was a young Guardian. A few of us tried to say them, but we could not figure out how to speak the words. It sounds like you and Rella may have been the first people in centuries to do so."

I took a deep breath and asked him the question that had been bothering me for so long.

"Master Em, do you think the chants could have damaged my Guardian powers? Do you think I can't heal anything because I did something bad? Because it messed me up . . . forever?"

Master Em stared up into the tree branches. Then he reached for the stick at his side and leaned on it to stand up. "You see this simple piece of fallen wood? Used in one way, it can be a walking stick for an old man."

With one swift motion, he swung the stick up in the air. He whipped it around in a circle and brought it down against the ground with a loud crack. I stared at him in amazement. In that moment he did not seem like an old man at all.

"Used in another way, this stick becomes a weapon," said Master Em. "But even then, it could be a weapon for defense or attack." He lowered the stick and leaned on it. "Few things in this world are completely bad or good. It's how we use them that determines the outcome."

I nodded. "I never used the chants to do anything bad. But I still worry that something is wrong with me. I'm turning out to be a complete failure as a Heart Guardian. I'm so different from the other Novices."

He leaned forward, his long beard hanging nearly to the ground. "Plum, look at me. Do *I* seem like anyone you've ever met?"

I smiled. "No, but it's different for me." I reached under my cloak for my shell pendant and held it up for him to see. "My mother had a dream for me, and she put it inside this shell. She wanted me to become a Guardian. I have to make her dream come true."

"Ah," said Master Em, nodding. "You want to fulfill your destiny."

"*Destiny?* What is that?"

"You want to become the person you are meant to be."

I sat up taller. "Yes! That's exactly what I want!"

"Destiny is a funny thing, Plum. When you're young, your future seems so cloudy and uncertain. But when you are my age and look back, the path of your life will be clear, like it was meant to be that way all along."

"No offense, Master Em, but that doesn't really help me right now."

He smiled. "You need to know your path. You want to find your destiny?" He transformed into the ginger ape and held out a leathery hand to me. "Well, then, help me help you find it."

I understood what he was asking. I transformed into the roan and bent my head. He placed his palm on my antlers and shut his eyes. I waited to feel our connection and then opened my eyes.

My stomach fluttered. What would his vision be for me?

"I see you . . ." said Master Em, his eyes still shut. "I see you coasting on the sea. You are moving so fast. You are traveling on an ancient road . . ."

I didn't understand—how could a road be on the sea? I leaned forward, listening.

"Ah, interesting . . . you are tracing the path of the Great Beast. You are making a wide circle, Plum . . . You will go all the way around . . ." Master Em smiled and laughed to himself. "Well, this is too funny."

"What is it? What do you see?"

"In the end, you will find that you held your destiny in your hands the whole time."

He opened his eyes and transformed back into an old man. I transformed back into my human self too.

"Master Em, I don't understand. Tracing the path of the Great Beast? That can't be possible. The Great Beast traveled here from the Old Home. That's all the way across the world. Are you sure you did your vision thing right?"

Master Em shrugged and leaned on his walking stick. "That's the thing about visions, Plum. They are crystal clear and muddy at the same time. All I know is that when I try to look at your future, I see nothing unless I look into the past. If you want to find your destiny, you will have to view these things as connected."

I sighed and looked out into the canopy of Bokati. "Connection. Just like the Bokati trees are connected to one another, I guess."

Master Em stretched his arms overhead and stood up. "It's not just the Bokati trees. We are all connected. You. Me. And the knobble shrooms."

He reached over to a cluster of knobble shrooms that

grew on the tree trunk. He tapped the tops of the mushrooms, sending a cloud of fine dust everywhere.

Instantly we started coughing.

"Ugh . . . these . . . spores!" Master Em coughed.

We waved our hands as we moved away from the spore cloud. My eyes watered. Pretty soon I was laughing and coughing at the same time.

"What is it?" asked Master Em.

"Well, I think it must have been destiny that you touched that knobble shroom."

"Oh really?"

I smiled. "Oh yes. It's given me a big idea."

CHAPTER 21

That night we gathered at the location of our next stake-out. So far Rella had followed a pattern, choosing trees in a spaced-out circle around the edge of the island. We decided to rely on this pattern again to predict where the next attack would be.

"Mikko, did you hide the supplies?" asked Master Em.

Mikko nodded and pointed to a large clump of ferns. "Over there, ready when we need them."

We were all quiet as the last light of day seeped away. I scanned the forest, hoping I would see Sam emerge from behind a tree in his wolfhund form.

Hetty put her hand on my shoulder. "Plum, I don't think we can wait any longer. He's not coming."

I took a deep breath. "Okay, I guess you're right. Ready, everyone?"

We all transformed into our Guardian forms and stood in a tight circle. Boosting everyone's powers one at a time took too long and made me too tired. I had an idea to do it all at once. Hopefully it would work.

Everyone held out their paw or hoof or wing and touched the Novice next to them until the whole circle was connected.

I took a deep breath and shut my eyes. It wasn't hard to picture all of us as connected. These were my dearest friends.

You, me, and the knobble shrooms, I thought.

My antlers thrummed like a pure note played on a piano. I could feel that electric tingle run through me, through Cherry, through Hetty, through each of us. This was stronger than anything I had felt before.

I opened my eyes. I felt so tired, and I hoped that was a good sign. I transformed back into my human form. My work was done.

We all looked at one another. Cherry, who had been standing next to me, was definitely bigger. Had it worked for everyone else?

Suddenly Hetty swung her head to the side. She wiggled her nose.

"I can feel it! Rella is close now."

"To your places, everyone," said Master Em. "Remember what we planned! Salan, here—the bag."

He held a sack out to Salan, who took it in his beak and flew up into the branches overhead.

We all went to our designated hiding spots to wait. I turned to Master Em and whispered, "Master Em, do you have any idea how this will turn out?"

He shook his head. "No, but I know for sure that we will put up a good fight."

We sat silently, listening. It was too dark to see my friends, but I knew they were there listening as well. Oh, how I wished we had Sam with us to hear the hoverbots approaching. But it wasn't long before I heard them myself: the buzzing like a thousand mechanical insects. Master Em held one finger to his lips, the sign to wait.

The buzzing grew louder. I felt the cool shadow mist creep in, making the darkness complete. Beside me, Master Em held still. *Not yet. Not quite yet . . .*

He tapped me with one finger. That was my cue.

I stood up and lifted my antlers high. I focused all my

energy there until they glowed red like coals in a fire. The forest became a ruby-colored haze.

"Now!" shouted Master Em.

Through the red haze, I saw the silhouettes of Mikko and Hetty. Mikko held his fans high and began to wave them. At the same time, Hetty stood up and hurled a large spherical object into the mist.

Thud!

It was the sweet sound of a pomelo rind hitting a hoverbot.

That afternoon we had carefully sliced open the pomelos and saved the rinds, filling them with knobble shroom spores. When our homemade pomelo bombs hit the hoverbots, they burst open, sending clouds of spores into the air.

The spore dust swirled in the air and stuck to the hoverbots. The bots, now covered in dust, became much easier to see.

"Take that, you crummy bots!" cried Mikko, waving his fans even harder to blow away the mist.

"Yeah, you can't hide from us now!" shouted Hetty.

I leapt out from my hiding spot and shone my antlers toward my friends. Cherry charged into the midst of the hoverbots. She grabbed one and swung it around and around, then released it into a cluster of others.

SMASH!

Yes! We all cheered.

I transformed back into my human form so I could help Hetty throw the pomelos. We threw them until they were all gone.

"It's working, look!"

Master Em lit his lantern and held it up high. The shadow mist was thinning, and the hoverbots were easily visible. Cherry picked them off one by one.

"She's going to need help," said Hetty.

"She's about to get it," I said. "Look up!"

High overhead we heard the flapping of Salan's wings. And then a large net of woven Bokati fibers dropped down onto the hoverbots, trapping them.

"Let's go finish them off," said Mikko. "Come on!"

Mikko leapt into the fray and shoved hoverbots this way and that. Hetty and Master Em followed.

Where was Rella? I listened. I could hear the sound of someone coughing. She must have been right in the thick of things when we threw the spore bombs. But even though the shadow mist had gotten thinner, I still couldn't see her.

Oh no! Would she get away? We couldn't let that happen!

I grabbed Master Em's lantern and ran toward the sound of the coughing. I still couldn't see her. When Rella was in her leopard form, she melted into the shadows. At night she would be practically invisible. And I was so tired. I couldn't even summon the energy to transform.

The sound grew fainter and fainter. I was going to lose her.

Suddenly an enormous shape lunged out of the trees toward me.

"Sam!" I cried when I realized who it was. "You found us!"

"I could smell you," he said with a grin. He knelt down so I could climb onto his back. "Now, come on, we can't let her get away!"

CHAPTER 22

I clutched the scruff of Sam's neck as he bounded this way and that through the trees. Every now and then, I heard a soft cough somewhere ahead of us. To Sam's super hearing, it must have been very loud.

He chased Rella all the way to the edge of the woods. We stopped where the trees met the beach. I slid off his back, and my feet crunched on the gravelly sand.

The sound of coughing was somewhere close to the water's edge. Sam growled, and then he pounced.

I held my lantern up as I jogged after him. Sam rolled across the gravel beach. It looked like he was wrestling with a shadow.

Finally the shadow vanished and the form of the gray

leopard appeared. Sam pinned the big cat down, growling above her.

Rella coughed repeatedly, and then she transformed back into her human form. She struggled to catch her breath.

"We can't let her go," said Sam, out of breath himself. "She'll run away."

But Rella didn't look like she could run anywhere. She was gasping for air, and she seemed weak and tired.

Sam stepped away from her and transformed back into his human form. "Explain yourself!" he shouted at Rella. "What are you doing with my mother's hoverbots? Did you steal them?"

Rella leaned on one elbow, panting. "Lady Ubon gave them to me so I could do a task for her."

"That's a lie!" cried Sam, with angry tears in his eyes.

I put my hand on his shoulder. "Rella, are you saying that Lady Ubon sent you on a mission to cut down the Bokati trees?"

Rella looked down at the sand. "She didn't say that *exactly*. But I knew she would be pleased if I got them for her."

"Do you have any idea how much damage you've done, Rella?" My voice cracked at the thought of the destruction I had seen.

"I chose trees that were far apart," she said. "My

calculations said I would only need six of them. I wasn't going to take any more than that."

"Calculations?" I asked, confused. "What are you using the trees for? Why did you take them?"

Rella started to answer, then closed her mouth tight when she looked at Sam. Whatever her reasons, she wasn't going to tell us anything.

"I spaced out the trees I took," said Rella, "so it wouldn't hurt the forest."

"The forest is more connected than you know," I said. "Those trees all share the same roots. If you had taken even one more, you could have killed them all."

Her eyes widened in shock, and then they filled with tears. "I didn't know! If I had known, I never would have agreed to take on this assignment."

Assignment? What was going on?

Sam was having none of it. "My mother would never have encouraged anyone to do something like this. You're just trying to pass the blame onto her because you're still upset about not making it into the Guardian Academy."

Rella's face hardened once more. "You can say whatever you want about me. I failed. It doesn't matter what happens to me next."

In the distance, we heard the voices of Master Em and the other Novices calling out for us.

"Master Em! We're over here!" said Sam. He looked at me. "Guard her and don't let her go anywhere."

He ran down the beach toward them, waving his arms to get their attention.

I knelt beside Rella, watching her. She was still the same fierce, tough girl I remembered. But something about her also seemed sad. I longed to ask her about the chants. Was she still using them? Was that how she had gotten so powerful? I wondered what kind of power I would have if I had kept speaking them.

Did this make us different from each other? Or did it make us the same?

She turned her face away. "Don't look at me like that," she said. "Like you feel sorry for me."

"I just don't understand you, Rella," I said.

She laughed, and it reminded me of how she had laughed when she'd teased me for being a simple farm girl. "Of course you don't understand," she said tauntingly. "You have no idea what it's like to be me. Now I don't have the Guardian Academy *and* I'll lose the favor of Lady Ubon too."

"So you *are* working for her?"

"Not anymore. She'll never keep me after a failure like this."

"So what are you going to do now?"

"I don't know," she whispered.

The voice of Master Em grew louder, and the others came running down the beach with him.

Suddenly Rella bolted to her feet and tried to run off. I grabbed her by the arm and held her tight.

"Let me go, Plum," she said. "I'm not going to let anyone else control my destiny. I'm going after it if I have to claw my way there."

Destiny.

The word jolted me like a shock. Rella was looking for her destiny. Just like I was.

I didn't know why I did it. I let my grip on her arm loosen and reached up to the shell pendant around my neck.

She seized her chance. She slipped away.

With one word of a whispered chant, the shadow mist enveloped her.

By the time the others got to me, she had vanished like smoke.

CHAPTER 23

The other Novices assumed Rella had fought me and escaped. Master Em gave me a funny look when I didn't correct them, but he didn't ask me any questions. I would never tell them the truth—that I had actually let her go. I couldn't explain why I had done it. I still didn't understand why myself.

When we returned to the attack site to clean up, Mikko examined the wrecked hoverbots. He figured out how to take the front panel off one of the bots and rewire it to send a message and a homing signal.

"That should alert the main control center back on Nakhon Island," said Mikko. "Lady Ubon will know where her hoverbots are now."

Sam nodded. "My mother will come here immediately. She'll be horrified to know her bots have been used in this way."

Lady Ubon arrived early the next morning on a sleek silver boat with mechanical sails.

Sam rushed into her arms when she stepped onto the beach. "Mother!"

She embraced him. "My darling! Thank goodness you're all right. The message you sent worried me so much." Lady Ubon turned to the rest of us and bowed to Master Em. "Words fail me," she said to him. "Please accept my deepest apologies. I had no idea that Rella had taken my hoverbots and used them in this way."

Master Em tilted his head at her. "Thank you, Lady Ubon. Do you have any idea why Rella would have done such a thing?"

"I cannot imagine. I gave her an assignment to find resources for a new project that would help the people of Nakhon Island. She must have misunderstood. I never meant for her to do something so destructive."

"Where are the trees that Rella and the hoverbots took away?" asked Salan.

"The Bokati wood has been harvested, and it is safely

stored in my warehouse back on Nakhon Island," said Lady Ubon. She quickly added, "The loss of the trees is a great tragedy, but it would be wasteful not to use their precious wood."

"What will you do with it all?" asked Hetty.

Lady Ubon smiled gracefully. "I am sure I can find some worthwhile use for it, something that will help the people of our islands. And, Master Em, I will program my hoverbots to plant fifty new Bokati trees for every one that was taken."

Master Em thanked her with a gruff nod. But we all knew that even if she planted a thousand new Bokati trees, it would take centuries for them to grow to the size of those that had been lost.

"Sam, come and walk with me," said Lady Ubon, holding her arm out to him. "I haven't seen you in a long time. I want to talk with you about something."

The two of them walked away along the shore. The rest of us helped Master Em gather pieces of Bokati driftwood that had washed up on the beach.

While Cherry and I worked, I pulled her away from the others. I whispered to her what Rella had told me about being here on an assignment for Lady Ubon.

Cherry wrinkled up her forehead. "I don't know, Plum.

Who is more likely to be lying, Lady Ubon or *Rella*? We already know that Rella has lied about stuff in the past."

"I guess that's true . . ."

"And think about it. Why would Lady Ubon tell Rella to come all the way out here to cut down Bokati trees? She has plenty of trees on Nakhon Island. She can have them anytime she wants."

But I had the feeling something didn't quite fit together. "Remember how Master Em said that Bokati wood is valuable?" I said. "It's unsinkable. What if Lady Ubon wants to build an unsinkable ship?"

Cherry waved her hand. "Lady Ubon has a whole fleet of ships. Super fancy ones. I think you should let it go, Plum. Let's just be glad that Rella is finally gone, this time for good!"

I nodded. Cherry was right. I should be relieved. So why did I feel like something had been left unfinished?

Sam came running up to us. "Plum, Cherry! My mother has had the most amazing idea! She's invited the two of you to spend the New Year holiday next month at our house on Nakhon Island!"

Lady Ubon followed behind him. She held her hand out to Cherry. "Girls, you have become such dear friends to my son. And since you both live so far away from Lotus Island, I imagine you won't be going home for the holiday."

It was true. The boat ticket home would be so expensive I didn't think my grandparents would be able to afford it.

Cherry pumped Lady Ubon's hand up and down excitedly. "Are you kidding? You bet your knobble shrooms we'll be there!"

Lady Ubon held her hand out to me, and I shook it. I looked up into her eyes.

Cherry had a point about not trusting Rella. But something made me not quite trust Lady Ubon either. Should

I go and stay with her? I looked at Sam. He was smiling so happily. I couldn't let my friend down.

"We would be delighted to join you, ma'am," I said. "Thank you for the invitation."

Cherry threw her arms around Sam's neck and mine. "New Year! The three of us are going to *party*!"

Hetty, Mikko, and Salan joined us.

"And since the rest of us live on Nakhon Island," said Hetty, "we can all meet up!"

We laughed and danced together in a circle.

"Come, children," said Lady Ubon. "I can give you all a ride back to Lotus Island on my boat."

We turned to Master Em and bowed to him with respect. And then we surrounded him and hugged him tight.

"Thank you for everything, Master Em," said Sam.

Hetty wiped away a tear. "You know what? I'm going to miss this damp, cold, gloomy island."

"Right?" said Mikko. "I think we got the best field study assignment of all."

"Does this mean we passed our test with you?" asked Salan.

"With flying colors," said Master Em with a wink.

Cherry patted Master Em's arm. "You never did get to see us wrestle. I guess that means you'll have to come visit us on Lotus Island."

Master Em smiled. "I am long overdue for a visit."

I clasped both of the old man's hands in mine. I didn't think he would ever leave his post as protector of the Bokati trees. I wondered if I would ever see him again. "Master Em, I'm going to carry your words with me forever."

He squeezed my hands tight. "I don't even need a vision to know that you will, my dear Plum."

We boarded Lady Ubon's boat. The mechanical sails rose, and the wind pushed us out to sea. The six of us stood at the back rail, watching the mountainous trees of Bokati Island vanish in the mist.

We leaned in close to one another, shoulder to shoulder, as the boat sped back to Lotus Island. I shut my eyes and felt my friends' warm presence. I wasn't using my powers, but I still felt that golden connection running through us all.

LEGENDS OF LOTUS ISLAND

Turn the page for a special sneak peek of

Plum's very first adventure!

Worms always think they know everything.

"Come on, friends, not there by the squash. You want to be over here by these chai-melons, trust me." I scooped the worms out of the dark, fluffy soil and set them down near the chai-melon vine. "There. Now make that dirt good and soft, because I want to eat some big, fat melons this summer."

I stood up and walked around our garden. The eggplant and crisp-cumbers were doing great this year. And of course our chili plants and snake beans were growing wild, as always. But my main concern was our fruit trees. This year I was determined that we would have *everything*: jackfruit, mangoes, tea fruit, rose apples, even stinky durian.

I heard a rustling in the mango leaves. "Oh, sorry to wake you," I whispered to the family of fox bats that hung upside down, sleeping. "Now, don't forget what we agreed. You get the mangoes up top and leave the low stuff for us, okay?"

The mama fox bat yawned and shut her eyes again. A couple of years ago they nibbled bites out of every mango on our tree. But now that I'd convinced Grandpa to take down the nets, they only took the fruit that was too high for us to reach.

In a couple of weeks it would all start getting ripe. I could practically taste the feast in my mouth. The only fruit we could never seem to grow was—

"Plum!"

I turned around to see Grandma shuffling down the hill toward me. "Over here in the orchard, Grandma!"

"Plum," she huffed, "come on up to the house, dear."

"Is everything okay?"

"Of course it is!" she said, but I saw the corner of her mouth twitch. She always did that when she wasn't telling me the whole story.

I wondered what was going on, but I knew better than to pester her.

I let her lean on my shoulder as we walked slowly back up the hill to our house. The cool evening breeze felt so good after a long, sweaty day working in the garden. As always, we paused in the one spot where we could see the entire island. Our little wooden house and barn stood at the top of the hill. The garden and orchard were down below, near the freshwater spring. On the other side, Grandpa's rice fields sloped down to the coconut grove. And all around, the blue ocean sparkled.

The sun was starting to set. The fox bats were waking up, and the swallows were already swooping overhead. I imagined them calling out to us: *Day is done! Day is done! Time for night!*

"Good night!" I called up to them. "Don't forget our deal about the mangoes!"

Out on the water, I spotted the little blue postal boat zipping back toward Big Crab Island. My stomach did a flip. We almost never got mail. I glanced at Grandma for some hint as to what was going on, but her face was like a stone.

Before we got to the house, Grandma patted my hand. "Oh, and tomorrow, remind me that I need your help with the wheelbarrow. The chai-melon bed is full of rocks, and we've got to move them so the worms can get in."

I looked back at the garden and shook my head. Those worms were never going to let me hear the end of this.

When we got inside, Grandpa was bouncing around the kitchen. "Plum, come! Sit down!" Our little velvet goat, Tansy, was hopping about, almost as energetic as he was.

He pulled out a chair for me and poured himself a cup of tea, sloshing it onto the table.

Tansy clip-clopped over and put her soft head in my lap. "Grandpa, what's going on? Why are you so excited?"

Grandma sighed and went to the stove to stir the soup. Her face looked like she'd sucked on a bitter lemon.

Grandpa patted my knee. "Plum, you know how we've talked about you spending more time around other people?"

"Yes," I said, still confused. "Is this about that summer camp on Big Crab Island?"

Grandma clanged her spoon against the pot. "Just tell her already."

Grandpa reached inside his jacket pocket and brought out an envelope. "Read it for yourself, my dear."

Dear Miss Plum,

I have the pleasure of inviting you to the Guardian Academy on Lotus Island. For centuries, the Guardians have fulfilled their ancient duty to protect and nurture life in the Santipap Islands. Every ten years, a new class of Novice Guardians is selected to train with our Masters. Your application identified you as a strong candidate to join the next Novice class. Please arrive on the full moon to begin the first phase of your training.

Sincerely,

Master Sunback

My mind tumbled around in a confused mess.

Tansy started nibbling the paper. "Stop that!" I jerked it

out of her mouth. "Grandpa, this must be a mistake. I didn't apply to the Guardian Academy."

He grinned. "I applied for you."

I sat straight up. "What! And you didn't tell me?"

"I didn't think you'd get in!" He cleared his throat. "What I mean is . . . I didn't want you to get your hopes up in case it didn't work out."

"But I . . . I can't be a Guardian. Those people are *magical*. They travel all over the islands doing . . . I don't know, magical stuff!"

Grandpa waved his fingers at me. "They all started off as regular kids."

"They transform into spectacular creatures," I said. "Like hywolves and zorahawks and—"

"Gillybears," offered Grandma.

I threw my hands up. "And gillybears! Can you imagine me as a gigantic white bear diving into the waves? It's ridiculous!"

"That's what the Academy is for—to learn." Grandpa leaned over to take my hand. "Plum, your Grandma and I have been talking about this for some time. You are such a special girl, and that is becoming clearer the older you get. You have such a way with plants and animals. You talked to those fox bats, and now we finally get to our enjoy our mangoes."

I rolled my eyes. "It's not like they *actually* understood me."

"Well, you can't spend your whole life here, being a farmer on this little island. You are meant to do great things. I know it!"

I looked at Grandma, but she had turned her back to me.

So they had been talking about me in secret? It would have been nice if they had let me in on this decision. I folded my hands in my lap. "Thank you, Grandpa, but I don't want to go," I said quietly.

"Plum, don't be silly. Think of the opportunity—"

"I'm not going!" I stood up. "Grandpa, if I'm gone, who will take care of the garden? Who'll take care of Tansy? Who will—"

Take care of you? I thought.

Grandma set the soup pot down on the table with a loud clatter. "Dinner's ready."

Tears welled up in my eyes. How could they expect me to eat when they had just turned my whole world upside down?

"I'm not hungry!" I yelled. I bolted out the door and into the night.

I ran out onto the grass with Tansy at my heels. The sky was deep purple now, and the stars had come out.

I wiped my cheeks and dribbling nose. Tansy put her head in my wet hand. That's one good thing about velvet goats—they don't care if you get snot on their ears.

"They want me to leave, Tansy. Can you believe that? And me, a Guardian? What are they thinking?"

I had seen a Guardian only once in my life, when we took the boat to Big Crab Island. She was there to heal their hundred-year-old fig tree that had been struck by lightning. In human form, she was so elegant and powerful that I'd thought she must be royalty. Before our eyes, she had transformed into a slinky gleamur. She had scrambled up into the branches and placed her hands on the blackened trunk. A bright light had streamed out of the crack, and the tree was healed.

"I can't do anything like that, Tansy. Look at me! I'm dirty. I'm barefoot. I'm—"

"Talking to a goat."

I turned around to see Grandma. I sniffled. "Talking to Tansy doesn't mean I have powers."

"Maybe." Grandma sighed. "But your grandpa is right, Plum. You *are* special. You don't know it because you've hardly ever left this island and you've got two crusty old people for friends. But there is something about you. I've known it for a long time."

"I don't care if I'm special. I don't want to go."

"I don't want it either," said Grandma quietly. "Plum, I think it's time I give you something." She reached into her apron pocket and brought out a small object. She placed it on my palm.

"A snail shell?" The coils of the honey-colored shell formed a slender, pointed cone. A string of fishing twine ran through a tiny hole in the top.

"Your mother made this when you were still in her belly."

My heart leapt like a grasshopper to hear Grandma talk

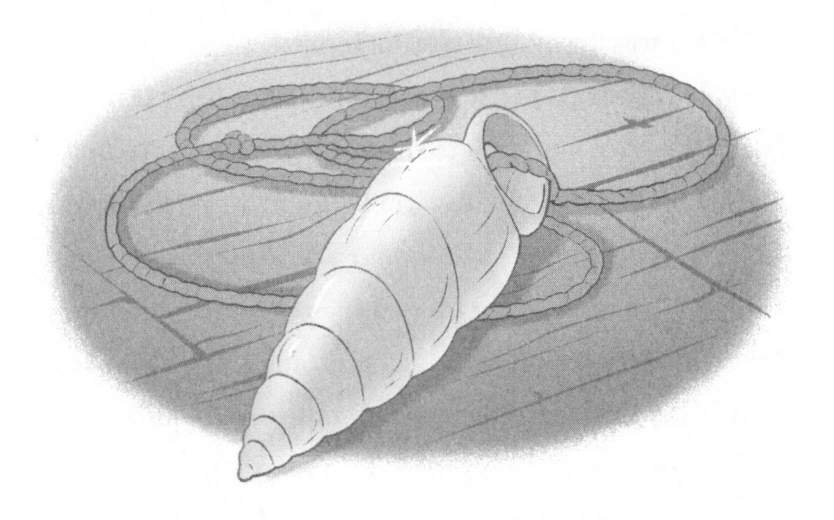

about my mother. I'd never known my parents. I was just a baby when a storm capsized their boat on the open sea.

"She made it after she had a dream about you. She said that she held tight to that dream and put it right inside this shell for you to have when you grew up." Grandma smiled. "I know you're not quite grown. But it's time for you to have it."

I gently traced the coils with my finger. I had always felt like I knew my dad, because Grandma's house was filled with his pictures and old toys. I even slept in his old bed. But we had only one photograph of my mother. I never asked questions about my parents because I didn't want to make Grandma sad. But now it felt like Grandma had opened a door. I had to hurry before it shut again.

"What was my mother like, Grandma?"

"When your dad first brought her here from Nakhon Island, I wasn't sure what to think of her. She was so quiet and small. But she took to farm life right away! She loved to work in the gardens beside your dad. And she loved the sea. They swam together every day after work. Sometimes I thought they would turn into seals and swim away, so I always made something good for dinner to lure them back home."

We both laughed at that.

"I've always thought it was cool that she was from Nakhon Island," I said. "It's such a big, fancy place."

"I'm afraid I don't know much about her life there. She didn't talk about her family, which made me think her past was a sad story. I didn't want to pry. I thought I would have so much more time to get to know her. Now I wish I hadn't waited."

Grandma took both my hands and held them tight like a clamshell. "She loved you so much. So did your dad. They'd both be so proud of how you are growing up."

Grandma was never this talkative. I hung on every word.

"Plum, we have done the best we can for you," she said. "We raised you how your parents would have wanted. But now I think it's time for you to see more of the world. I think they would have wanted that too."

I looked out at the moonlit waves. Our island was perfect in every way. But I also felt something tugging at me, like the tide. As much as I hated to admit it, there was something in me that was curious to go.

"But Grandma . . . being a Guardian? Only a few people ever learn how to do that. What if I can't?"

She squeezed my hand. "Then you'll come back here. This will always be your home. But if you don't try, you'll never know what might have been. Plum, you have—gah! Tansy, get off me!"

Tansy ripped off a chunk of Grandma's apron and swallowed it down.

"Can you take this dang goat with you when you go?"

We both laughed again.

"Here." Grandma took the snail shell out of my hand. "It may look fragile, but it's actually very tough and strong. Just like your mother. Just like you." She tied the twine around my neck, then cupped my face in her steady hands. I tried not to cry because I knew Grandma never did. "This is the right thing to do, Plum. I can feel it in my bones."

I shut my eyes. I wanted to feel it too, but I still wasn't sure. I listened to the night bugs and the frogs singing all around us. I imagined them saying, *Give it a try, give it a try, give it a try.*

"Okay," I said. "I'll give it a try."

CHAPTER 4

"You have your boat ticket?" asked Grandpa as we walked down the hill to our little wooden dock.

"Yes, Grandpa."

"And your jacket?"

"Yes, Grandpa."

"And your hat? Socks? Oh, what about extra underwear?"

"Grandpa!"

My grandma cut him off. "Stop fussing so much. The girl is bringing enough stuff to open her own market! Now, Plum, don't forget this."

She handed me a basket covered with her handkerchief. "I made extra honey egg cakes." She squeezed my hand.

"You can share them with the other kids during the boat ride. Make some new friends."

The large passenger boat swung up beside our dock, and its motor idled, chugging loudly. I had never been on a boat so big before. I grasped the shell pendant around my neck.

"Grandma? What do you think my mother dreamed for me?"

"I don't know," said Grandma softly. "But maybe while you're on Lotus Island, you'll discover the answer."

I threw my arms around her and hugged her tight. Her hair smelled like sweet dough and ginger. "Thank you, Grandma." Then I hugged Grandpa, and he squeezed me so hard it made me laugh. "I love you, Grandpa!"

"Go on, hurry, now," said Grandma. "You don't want to make them wait. And always remember that we—gah! Tansy! How'd you get out of your pen?" She shooed Tansy away from her apron. "Please take this goat with you!"

I nuzzled Tansy one last time. "Take care of them, girl."

I ran down the dock, suitcase in one hand, basket in the other. Before I knew it, I had handed over my ticket and my luggage, and we were shoving off. I stood at the rail and watched as my island became smaller and smaller behind us.

"Goodbye! Goodbye! I love you!"

ABOUT THE AUTHOR

Christina Soontornvat is the bestselling author of two Newbery Honor books, *A Wish in the Dark* and *All Thirteen: The Incredible Cave Rescue of the Thai Boys' Soccer Team.* She is also the author of Scholastic's beloved fantasy series Diary of an Ice Princess, the graphic novel *The Tryout*, as well as the picture book *To Change a Planet.* As a child, Christina spent most of her time at her parents' Thai restaurant with her nose stuck in a book. These days, she loves nothing better than spending a day hiking and swimming in the creeks and swimming holes around Austin, Texas, with her husband and two daughters. You can learn more about her work at soontornvat.com.